# Genaro González

Arte Publico Press
Houston
Texas
1991

This volume is made possible through a grant from the National Endowment for the Arts, a federal agency.

The author would like to thank the National Endowment for the Arts for a Creative Writing Fellowship which allowed completion of this manuscript.

The following stories originally appeared elsewhere: "The Heart of the Beast" and "Real Life" in *Riversedge*; "Too Much His Father's Son" in *The Denver Quarterly*; and "Home of the Brave" in *A Texas Christmas: Volume II.*

Arte Publico Press
University of Houston
Houston, Texas 77204-2090

Cover design by Mark Piñón
Photograph by Evangelina Vigil-Piñón

González, Genaro, 1949–
    Only sons / by Genaro González.
        p.    cm.
    ISBN 1-55885-031-7
    1. Mexican Americans—Families—Fiction.    2. Fathers and sons—Fiction    I. Title.
PS3557.047405 1991
813'.54–dc20                                        91-4679
                                                         CIP

The paper used in this publication meets the minimum requirements of the American National Standard for Permanence of Paper for Printed Library Materials Z39.48-1984. ∞

Para mi esposa, Elena.

# CONTENTS

Real Life . . . . . . . . . . . . . . . . . . . . . . . 9

Home of the Brave . . . . . . . . . . . . . . . 28

Frontier . . . . . . . . . . . . . . . . . . . . . 43

Too Much His Father's Son . . . . . . . . . . . 58

Old Acquaintances . . . . . . . . . . . . . . . 68

The Heart of the Beast . . . . . . . . . . . . . 88

Boys' Night Out . . . . . . . . . . . . . . . . . 107

Independence Day . . . . . . . . . . . . . . . . 116

# Only Sons

# Real Life

The phone call, Ernesto had been told, was from home. "It's Mrs. Aguirre," said an apprentice welder. There was just one problem: Ernesto was single. It must be Yolanda, he thought correctly, as he took the call in a corner of the auto body shop.

"Sorry I burned you," she said. "But I figured this was the surest way to get the message through. If they only knew ... "

"That I'm living with an older woman?"

"Well, maybe he thought I was your mother."

Even over their bad connection Ernesto caught the nervous edge in her voice. Besides, she'd only call if it were important.

"What is it?" he asked.

She took a deep breath and the static seemed to get worse. "Your uncle Lázaro just called. Your aunt took a turn for the worse."

"How much worse?"

"She's in a coma."

She waited for a reply until she thought they had been disconnected. "Ernesto. Are you still there?"

"Yes."

"If you want I can make something up for your boss."

"What for?"

"So you can be with your family."

Again it seemed the line had gone dead, until he asked, "But how would my being there help?"

"How could it hurt? Ernesto, they're practically your parents! The poor man completely forgot where you work. He called four beauty shops before finding me. Listen, I have to go. A client's under the dryer. So do you want me to talk to your boss?"

Glancing at his smudged coveralls he thought of the hospital's immaculate nurses, of its scrubbed silence, and felt the strength ebb from his limbs. The air hammers, and sanders inside the shop made it difficult to think. "No, I'll do it."

His foreman was under a station wagon, estimating repairs for a tense client. When Ernesto knocked on the rocker panel, the foreman poked his head out like an over-turned turtle in a metal shell, then rolled out on a mechanic's creeper.

His reaction to the news was an indifferent shrug. "An aunt, you say? We can't miss work for every *compadre* who wakes up with a hangover."

Ernesto felt compelled to explain, "I'm an orphan. My aunt and uncle raised me since I was one."

The foreman half-covered his mouth with his hand, then gave his consent with a pat on the back. Ernesto wondered whether the condolence was meant for his aunt or for his being orphaned.

Walking towards the parking area behind the shop, he noticed the blotted oil puddles where nothing grew. The stained sand felt like damp ashes under his feet, and for the first time in years he smelled the gasoline fumes that rolled in the stifling afternoon air and made the alley cats groggy. During the drive to the hospital, the fumes created a memory all their own, making his thoughts, return to the secure routine of the shop.

As he entered the hospital, in the main lobby he found the same volunteer from his last two visits.

"Enriqueta Flores," he said, pronouncing the name without softened, Anglicized syllables. "Room two-one-five."

He left while she still cross-checked her index file. "One moment, young man. The patient was transferred to the intensive care section."

He waited for the new number, then realized she had no intention of giving it. "And?"

"And," she said with icy efficiency, "only immediate family is allowed."

He stood agape, at first convinced she had noticed he stood out from his ruddy uncle and cousins. Then he caught her staring at his chest pocket, where "Aguirre" had been stitched. He tried to explain but in the end became tangled in frustration.

Half an hour later, his uncle, don Lázaro Flores, left his wife's bedside to check downstairs and found Ernesto waiting meekly in the lounge. With his uncle leading him upstairs, the receptionist let him through.

"Who else is here?" Ernesto asked.

"Just you. Elvira had to leave the baby with her in-laws, and Polito disappeared as soon as he heard the news. The boys are searching for him."

He followed don Lázaro through a labyrinth of corridors, glimpsing into rooms where solemn relatives seemed to suffer as much as the patients. When they reached his aunt's room, don Lázaro paused at the door. "The doctor said she's already agonizing."

Ernesto entered cautiously, expecting a terrible moan at any moment. But when he dared his first look, she seemed worse than dead. A network of catheters kept her on this side of existence. He had anticipated something more reassuring, and the flimsy web of tubes only sealed his dread. Her face, ordinarily as dark and robust as his, appeared wan, as if dusted with powder. With her dark vigor gone, the wrath he had always read in her face now seemed as irrational as a childhood fear.

"She's so pale. So lifeless." He had meant it as a thought, then realized he had said it aloud.

"She's still my Prieta, my dark one." said his uncle.

An hour later they consulted a specialist who explained step-by-step why his prognosis showed no hope. He was candid without being cruel, and when he suggested they grant her the peace she deserved, Ernesto felt the peace of a well-reasoned argument. He agreed completely with the opinion and checked for don Lázaro's concurrence.

But the recommendation was so alien to the old man's thinking that he continued standing in polite attention, waiting for something to make sense. He could not understand how a man could so casually describe the facts of death.

Then, realizing that an answer was expected of him, he finally said, "I see." He managed a somber appearance, and remained so until the specialist left. Then he smiled, shook his head and cocked it in the doctor's direction, as though he had humored him all along. "Double-talk."

It was Ernesto's turn in the dark. "What?"

"Double-talk. They double the bullshit to justify padding their fees."

Taking his time, Ernesto rephrased the comment in language don Lázaro might better understand. But the old man would have none of it. Minutes later a small apparatus was wheeled in and they were asked to leave the room. When they finally went in, they found Enriqueta Flores with plastic bands on her arms and several cords connecting her to the machine.

Don Lázaro shook his head again. "More gadgets to add to the bill," he said.

Ernesto barely heard him. "Soon she'll be nothing but machines."

What do these boys know about *las cosas de la vida*? Let's bring Fela the healer. She'll teach them a thing or two." He vigorously patted Ernesto's shoulder. "You have to understand—these doctors care only about their money. They gave us the once-over and figured we're too poor to be soaked."

"Then why don't they just cure her?"

Don Lázaro thought for a moment. "They're just holding her hostage. The minute we show them more money they'll suddenly remember some wonder drug in back of a shelf somewhere."

"But, Tío," he said "it's hopeless."

Don Lázaro would have none of that. "You're a reasonable man, Neto. A good mechanic, but a bad miracle worker."

Ernesto looked long and hard at his aunt, then at the walls of the same hospital where his parents had passed away within minutes of each other. "Okay, show me a miracle and I'll believe."

"Elvira is our miracle." His uncle guided him to the door with a voice mellowed by memories. "For several years after we got married, your aunt and I couldn't have children. We consulted doctors on both sides of the border, but each one said the same thing—my Prieta was infertile." He paused and frowned. "But who finally cured her? Fela *la curandera*. We had searched far and wide and the answer was right in our own backyard. Twelve months after we contacted Fela, your aunt gave birth to a beautiful girl. Afterwards I took little Elvira to those doctors and said, 'Here's a little something for your books'. When the others came, I did the same thing."

He returned to his wife's side. "If my Prieta was able to give life, then it's nothing to bring her out of a dream."

Ernesto quietly stepped out of the room just as the elevator door opened and don Lázaro's four sons spilled out, arguing noisily. A head poked out of a room, shushing them to no avail.

Federico Flores, married for eight months, was already declaring that his mother, conscious or not, would hold his first child in her arms. No one questioned his arrogance.

Ernesto met them in the hall. "Where's Elvira?"

Polito, mumbled an incoherent reply as Federico said testily, "Who knows what goes on in her head? She wasn't the least bit disturbed by the news."

"What makes you say that?" asked Ernesto.

"She hasn't shed a tear."

"Have you?"

"Men don't cry. At least not the Flores men."

Despite Federico's boast, Polito was already staining the family honor. He daubed his eyes on the sleeve of his butcher uniform and the tears left watercolors where the blood of some beast had not yet caked.

Once inside the hospital room, Rodolfo, the youngest, stared at the tubes and catheters looking at the others as if they had kept the truth from him. "Is she still alive?" he asked just as Polito whispered "Will mama be all right?"

"How should I know, you ox?" Federico replied, "Do I look like a doctor?"

Ernesto approached the brothers. "The specialist says it's useless."

Polito turned his attention to him. "But there's always hope, right?"

"Even if she comes out of it, she'll be completely paralyzed. She won't even recognize us."

Manuel raised his palms. "Then it's all in God's hands."

"Not God's," said Ernesto. "Ours." They squirmed under the weight of his words. "It's best to give her the peace she deserves."

Federico locked eyes with him. "Who the hell asked you?"

"I'm just suggesting ... " He searched the others for support but found himself outside their closely-defined circle.

With slow, deliberate steps Federico stepped between Ernesto and the brothers, then forced out the words through clenched teeth: "You never gave a damn about our mother."

Don Lázaro gave a soft yet firm reprimand, "That's enough, Federico."

But, Federico continued. "You don't even hold a candle in this wake."

"Take it easy," said Manuel. "We shouldn't talk about mama like she's already dead.

"Manuel is right," said don Lázaro. "Now all of you be quiet. The last thing I want is Prieta waking up to quarrels."

* * *

He reached Yolanda's house, more exhausted than after his busiest days. Her son Juanito was still in school, and Yolanda was not yet home. That morning she had mentioned a backlog of appointments at the beauty shop.

Lying on her oversized sofa, his last recollection before shielding his face with a cushion was the Army portrait of her ex-husband behind the sofa, where Juanito had insisted on placing it. Several attempts later he could not shake the feeling that the man was keeping vigil; so, working one end at a time, he moved the sofa until he could not longer see the face on the picture.

Juanito did not get home until five. When asked to account for his whereabouts, he simply turned a deaf ear and went to watch television. By the time Yolanda arrived, Ernesto had already started dinner. "How is she?" was her first question. He shrugged without looking at her, and she added, "Your uncle sounded desperate."

"He's desperate because everything's at a standstill." Ernesto sounded as though he were not directly affected or involved. "It must be terrible feeling so helpless."

She gave him a perplexed stare. But he left it at that, so she changed the conversation. "Who moved the sofa?" When no one answered, she directed her comment at no one in particular. "I suppose it crept over by itself."

"It wasn't me!" said Juanito, pointing out that the sofa was too heavy for him to move. Ernesto then confessed.

"How come?" she asked.

"Our friend was getting to me." He indicated the portrait, with its romantic, homesick look capable of melting any mother or sweetheart.

"Don't make fun of my father! He killed a hundred guys in Vietnam."

Ernesto imitated the droopy gaze. "They must have died laughing," he said, throwing the boy into a tantrum.

"Enough! You're both acting like children."

Juanito, having every right to behave like one, simply smiled.

"The boy needs discipline, Yolanda." It was meant as

impartial advice; yet, he couldn't hide his disappointment. On moving in, Ernesto had been brimming with the best of paternal intentions, prompted by an affinity with the boy's situation. But these days, despite an occasional truce, they had become more rivals than relatives.

Yolanda ignored them and sat at the table with an exhausted sigh. "Three days before Easter all these middle-aged women want to be resurrected into raving beauties."

"If it weren't for them you'd be out of a job."

"That's not it. They were never attractive to begin with. Now they expect miracles."

He admired her large, brown eyes and her full lips, "They can't all mature like you."

"That's because I feed on tender young men." She glanced at her watch. "Anyway, I'm due back at the beauty shop. We have appointments until late. And after that I promised to talk to a client who's having boyfriend problems."

"So when will you be back?"

She replied nonchalantly, "When I get back."

"Why not confess you have a rich gringo across town?" he deadpanned.

Sucking her breath as if she had eaten too much chile, she came closer and purred, "What gave me away? Blond hairs on my brush?"

She tried to carry on the kidding, but seeing how he was really thinking about other things, she changed her tone. "I'm also doing this for you, Ernesto. I know you prefer being alone when you're worried."

In reality he had never wanted her more than tonight, but he lied. "I was going to visit Tía Queta anyway." It sounded like those ordinary evenings when he'd drop in on her in the old barrio where Yolanda's family lived.

She smoothed the wrinkles on her white uniform. "I

should change." She murmured something else, and Ernesto, catching her faraway look, made an inquiring gesture with his head. "I suddenly thought about the time after my divorce, when my sisters and I were living with mama. We'd all leave for work wearing our white uniforms, and later we'd all bring back the smells from our jobs. Cristina smelled liked the chicken and fish from the poultry plant. I was soaked in hair spray and perfume. And little Cynthia reeked with the medicine from the clinic, like the alcohol they rub on you before a shot. I get goose bumps just thinking about it." She raised a sleeve to show her arm.

He remembered seeing a cat once trailing after Cristina. He could not have been more than eight at the time. "How long has Cristina worked in the poultry plant anyway?"

"Only God's grandmother knows. In time everyone said the white uniform made her feel like a perpetual bride."

"How can you talk about your own family that way?"

"What way?"

"Aren't you ... ashamed she never got married?"

She would have laughed out loud if he hadn't sounded so serious. "Most of us scramble on the boat but afterwards can't get off." She patted her hips to congratulate herself. "A few of us risk jumping overboard." Then she added with a hint of gossip, "You'd never guess to look at Cristina, but she's had her fun."

"What a liar! No one's pointed a finger at her for as long as I can remember."

She imitated him, "For as long as I can remember," and leaned over to pinch his nostrils as though wiping snot from his face. "Do you remember this too: who used to change your diapers?"

She was referring to one of don Lázaro's anecdotes, based partly on fact. This much was certain: little Yolanda, living three houses from the Flores family, had been fascinated by their "new baby boy," and had visited him every day for over a month. Beyond that, the account was at best apocryphal. Whether she had actually carried Ernesto in her arms, much less helped change him, was something no one could confirm.

He picked his food. "No doubt you sprinkled some special baby powder on me when you were squeezing the goods. That's why I ended up with you."

*       *       *

That evening he returned to the hospital and came upon don Lázaro murmuring at his wife's bedside. Taking a chair from the other side of the partition he noticed a very old woman asleep on the other bed. Shriveled, with the color of an unearthed mummy, she might have looked more at home in a museum.

Certain that his uncle was praying, he sat to one corner in quiet respect. Then at one point don Lázaro chuckled, and Ernesto realized his uncle had been conversing all along. "Is something wrong, Tío?"

Don Lázaro shook his head, then confided, "I was reminding Prieta of that electrical storm that took place the year we worked in North Dakota. She ran from child to child, covering their heads to protect them from the lightning. By the time she reached you, we were out of towels and aprons. And your black hair—even thicker than Prieta's—made you a walking lightning rod. So she wrapped your head in my striped boxer shorts, like a turban. We all laughed till we cried. Except Polito, who cried for real because you reminded him of the evil gypsies in the movies."

He could not remember the incident, but smiled anyway to humor his uncle. Suddenly don Lázaro made a slight gesture toward his wife.

"She moved her finger!" he whispered. "The one with the wedding ring."

Without thinking, Ernesto turned in his aunt's direction, gasping as he heard a voice say, "Liar! I never set foot in North Dakota!"

For an instant he stared, astonished, at his aunt. Don Lázaro read his thoughts. "It's only the woman in the other bed," he said defeated.

"I never worked a day in North Dakota!" the woman insisted in her delirium, then quickly added, "Now Michigan is another story. Fruit trees as far as the eye can see. Money grows on trees, but the catch is the bitter cold mornings. Harvest cold cash you might say—."

Don Lázaro shook his head. "She's been that way since she arrived."

Ernesto still scrutinized his aunt's mouth on the chance she had thrown her voice. He shuddered. "It sure sounded like Tía."

Don Lázaro scratched the stubble on his chin.

"So what should I do, my son?"

There was something peculiar about the question. Then it became clear: It was one of the few times don Lázaro had called him "son." Ernesto could not meet him on the same terms. "It's your decision, Tío."

Don Lázaro removed his spectacles with the caution of someone peeling off a painful adhesive. He covered his face, and for a moment seemed about to cry. But he merely rubbed the sleep plaguing his eyes. Focusing back on Ernesto, his face seemed startled and childlike without the glasses. Only the bridge of his nose, where spectacles had left a yoke through most of his fifty-odd years, showed the markings of age.

"I've meant to bring this up for so long, Netito. I'm even embarrassed ... " He looked away then glanced back abruptly. "It's about one's love for one's family. Do you understand? ... No, how could you?"

All at once Ernesto felt empty. In one breath don Lázaro had estranged him not just from the family but from all of humanity. Bracing his trembling voice, he protested, "But you've loved me like a son. You even called me that now."

"We tried. At first Prieta even said you were the over-due baby from those childless years. It became a family-saying that you took so long in coming because as migrants we were always one state ahead of the stork. But then ... you started growing up."

"I hardly ever gave you any trouble."

"That's true. Compared to the others you were a model child. And the few times you disobeyed, my Prieta did the punishing, since she was your mother's sister. I felt I had no say in those matters, much like you've told me about Yolanda's little boy. Besides, I never had the heart to dis-cipline children, not like my Prieta." He paused, then added with nostalgia, much like the tone he had used to address his comatose wife, "But in all those years, there was something missing. I remember the times when one of the kids would start acting silly, and the rest of the family would catch it, even Prieta. Then I'd laugh in your direction and be met by that distant look—like someone looking in from the outside." He turned to his wife. "You sensed it too, didn't you?"

*   *   *

He entered Yolanda's house with the surreptitious cau-tion of a burglar. Taking the television into the bedroom, he selected a channel at random. The volume control worked erratically, resulting in an increasing loudness so that the set had to be turned off, then on again.

He renewed a personal pledge to have it repaired. A wedding gift from Yolanda's in-laws, he had first avoided watching the TV out of a vague and misplaced pride. In time he had outgrown the discomfort of living with someone's ex-wife. But today, lying on the stranger's bed, watching his television, he felt once more that he was inheriting another man's hand-me-downs.

He watched television until his eyes grew numb. When the station went off the air, he turned off the ceiling light and let the static play with his thoughts. Lulled by the hiss, he curled up and fell asleep. Twice he woke up, staring at the slight figure huddled beside him without recognizing her.

When he woke up the next morning, Yolanda had left him a portion of scrambled eggs. He preferred them hard-boiled, but Easter was two days away and for a month she had been saving the shells for Juanito to decorate. As an act of good faith, Ernesto had done without hard-boiled eggs in order to increase Juanito's collection.

Yolanda apologized for getting home so late, then teased, "You left the set on last night."

"I fell asleep in the middle of a movie."

"Strange. You hate television." She suppressed a smile, then confessed: "When Juanito was a baby, my mother-in-law had him spoiled something terrible, insisting I carry him at every whimper. So I began turning on the TV beside his crib, without the sound. In ten minutes he'd be asleep, and if he woke up, the morning images would put him to sleep again."

"No wonder he's addicted to the thing," he said as he ate his breakfast.

Yolanda waited 'til he finished eating before asking about his aunt. He took his time answering. "It's Tío Lázaro I'm more worried about. He only has fond memories of her. To hear him talk you'd think he was describing someone else."

"How do you remember her, Neto?"

He almost began discussing his uncle again, then he paused.

"She was ... stern ... strict." He knitted his brows. "I even ran away from home once because of her."

"I remember! We still lived a few houses down. The barrio organized a search party. That night they caught me kissing behind Bernal's store. You didn't turn up until the next morning."

"I spent the night under the house."

"Why there?!"

"Tía Queta always said that was the Devil's hideout. So I made a pact: I'd stay there all night provided he'd take her afterwards." Immediately, he became silent.

Yolanda distracted him with some calculations. "You couldn't have been more than seven. Weren't you terrified?"

"Just once. I didn't know I'd picked the dog's sleeping place, and all of a sudden this panting, furry thing was all over me. I saw those glowing eyes and nearly passed out! Afterwards he kept me company." For a moment he actually heard the family's muffled voices and footsteps creaking just inches over his face. "All this time someone was weeping above, and I told myself, 'This is what it's like being buried.'"

Yolanda met his gaze. "It was her." He seemed confused. "It was your aunt Queta crying." From her expression he did not know if Yolanda had made it up.

"That's a poor guess."

"It's no guess. Cristina was there. That was the only time anyone saw her cry."

They began clearing the table in silence. All at once he said, "I don't want her to die." The remark carried a stubborn simplicity, like the pure and absolute faith children put behind an impossible wish.

Yolanda prepared him for the worst. "If she does, at least her ordeal will be over."

"That's only the beginning."

"What do you mean?"

"As a kid I never worried about Tío or Tía discovering my wrongdoings. Covering my tracks there was easy. But I'd imagine my real parents watching my every move, even knowing my thoughts. The dead discover our worst side, you know, and we have to live with their disappointment."

"Those were childhood superstitions, Neto! Don't tell me you still believe them."

He reminded her of the last two anniversaries of her father's death, when she had put a moratorium on their lovemaking.

"That's different," she protested. "That was a matter of respect. But, once you move below ground, you can't even feel the rats gnaw."

\*   \*   \*

By the time he reached the hospital that morning, Elvira and the Flores brothers were already with don Lázaro. Next to his aunt's bed a new apparatus had been added. Manuel caught his gaze and nodded toward his father, who was muttering next to the bed. Ernesto crouched beside his uncle.

"And remember, Prieta, the time we were returning from the fields in the back of the Menchacas' truck? You were scolding Elvirita for balancing herself on crates in order to look over the railings, when splat! They ran over a dead skunk!" He shuddered slightly as he stifled his laughter. "For the rest of the way we had to join her, looking over the railing like the dogs of rich gringos that stick out their snouts from the car window."

"That was no dead skunk!" said the old woman in the next bed. "We were passing a cabbage patch!"

Federico, staring out the window, had grown a mustache of sweatbeads. "Doesn't she ever shut up? Bad enough that papa babbles to himself without her encouragement." He approached the old woman and just inches from her face he said, "Hush, *señora*!"

"A cabbage patch!" she insisted, then just as abruptly, "I mean a cemetery for rich skunks!"

"Hush!"

"You hush," said Elvira. "Better to have one person hallucinating than two carrying on a conversation."

In a moment of lucidity don Lázaro said, "Leave her in peace. She's just lonely."

"It makes me furious," said Federico. "Mama will never say another word, and here this old parrot won't stop talking."

"Your mother talks too," said don Lázaro. "You just don't listen." He placed a hand on his son's shoulder and gently led him to one corner. Their conversation reached Ernesto in mumbles until Federico said he was leaving.

After the others were gone too, don Lázaro gave a sardonic smile. "How right you were, Netito. Now even Federico's against me. 'That's all she wrote,' he said."

Ernesto pointed toward the machines. "Nowadays they can work wonders."

"Perhaps." He shrugged. "Perhaps it's only done with mirrors." He seemed exhausted. "Will you be at Yolanda's?"

When Ernesto nodded a timid yes, don Lázaro appeared to consult his wife, then he clasped his hands and put them behind his neck. "I'm seeing the specialist in an hour. By noon you'll have my decision."

"There's no hurry, Tío."

"My Prieta wants it that way." He moved towards her with a stiff movement, only to draw back when he came too near. He folded his arms across his abdomen as if his stomach hurt.

\*   \*   \*

When the noon hour passed without a call, Ernesto reasoned that his uncle had lacked the nerve. He turned on the television, lay on the bed and gave in to a pleasant numbness, here and there catching scenes of a poorly acted melodrama about two star-crossed lovers. By the last scene the volume became so loud that the tender affair degenerated into a shouting match. But by then he was almost dead to the world, trying to string chaotic images into a coherent dream.

The phone rang, barely audible above the fracas, yet he sprang to his feet as though he had been waiting in silence and with all his senses alert. For some time he stood in the center of the room without moving to answer the phone. The persistent ringing could only come from a caller who expected someone home.

He walked toward the TV, to turn it off out of respect for his uncle's pronouncement. Then he stooped and pressed his forehead against the screen to drown out the phone.

The sorrow of the screen lovers had transcended speech, and a solitary saxophone wailed out the last notes of bathos. He found solace in the noise. In real life such moments did not even merit a cheap tune, only an overwhelming silence which amplified one's aloneness.

And still the phone rang. Perhaps his uncle, in a change of heart, had decided to let her live. But that fiction could last only for as long as the truth were delayed.

He imagined his uncle counting the echoes with infinite patience, while Ernesto let each ring take him farther away from the inevitable.

If only the phone rang long enough ...

# Home of The Brave

So far his flight back to the States had been a series of stand-bys. The usual holiday crowds had congested every terminal from Honolulu to Houston, but by some miracle of the season he had not been bumped off. By now he realized that his fear of standing out in uniform was unfounded: servicemen of every size, rank and hue swarmed the airports, so that the departure lobbies seemed at times scattered suburbs of Saigon. The closer he got home, the more homogeneous their faces, until only other *raza* and an occasional redneck prevailed. And it was their unquestioning attitude of the unentitled—that whatever came their way was a duty to see through—that made him question his own uncertainty even more.

He was in South Texas now. God's country, they said, by default, because the Devil would have no part of it. Here the stories of spat-on soldiers seemed as remote as the war he had left only days behind. Here one crossed paths with walking anachronisms: Anglo hyperpatriots who could pass for unwashed squatters of an earlier century, and Chicanos who still had that immigrant optimism that their own grandfathers had grown old anticipating. The President could not have asked for a more blindly loyal following. His flight south slowly turned into a time warp of tranquility.

The last leg was Tex-Mex territory, which made the Anglo soldier across the aisle appear like the beleaguered, sole survivor of a last stand. He kept fidgeting with his sling as though nursing an irritable infant. The only gringo grunt he had seen south of the Nueces, and he had gotten himself shot. He almost wished his own wound were more conspicuous. With all the dead and maimed being sent back, returning visibly intact seemed more a sin than good fortune. Well, he consoled himself, some scars don't show; then he smiled. He was already falling back on cliches, an essential weapon on re-entering society.

The memory of that precise instant seventeen days ago seemed infinitely more vivid than the sedate reality surrounding him. In purely objective terms, it had occurred on the seventh of December, at 09:38 Saigon military time, this last detail courtesy of the projectile that creased his back-side and smashed a wristwatch bought on the black market a month earlier. In purely subjective terms, his immediate reaction, even before the automatic groin check, had been the certainty that, for better or worse, he would be home for Christmas. Everything else—whether his tour in Nam was all over, or whether his entire tour on earth was truly finished—was, in his father's words, for the history books.

The comments of the corpsman who had attended his injury were less metaphysical. "You're one lucky Tex-Mex, Ortiz. That wild round barely kissed your ass. An inch or two and you'd be selling Girl Scout cookies. You'll get the Purple Butt for sure, sit out the rest of your tour. Well, maybe sit out's not the right phrase. But the main thing is you're going home, my man."

He had clenched his teeth, not from pain but to keep

them from chattering. "But Uncle Sam'll still own my ass!"

"That's a roger," promised the corpsman. "I'll patch it up new as a baby's butt." He had finished dressing the wound. "So go back to the world. Just don't get too comfortable. We're not through with you yet."

When he saw his relatives huddled at the arrival gate, he almost cursed his parents under his breath. They understood his idiosyncratic solitude well, but for twenty-odd extroverts to honor his request was asking too much. Most had never been inside an airport, and the novelty only added to the chaos.

Suddenly everyone was embracing him, and not until the end did he notice an absence. "And Tío Plácido?"

"Your uncle couldn't make it," said his mother.

His first thought was that he had gone back to the veteran's hospital. "I could have called him during my stopover in San Antonio ... "

"Oh, he's home." She lowered her voice to avoid any direct accusations. "But the boys started celebrating your arrival."

"Everyone knows he can't ... !" He caught himself and said nothing more.

Neither did he say much when the caravan regrouped at his parents'. He did catch a few asides on his silence. "Must be exhausted from the trip," said one aunt.

Another added, "Tila's boy came back the same way. He's fine now."

In the living room he confronted his portrait, placed in his absence and flanked by the full-faced, three-dimensional woodcut of his father and a more modest, achromatic oval of his uncle, all three in uniform. He had sat for it in Garza's studio the day he received his orders. The same photographer had chronicled family baptisms, first communions and graduations, becoming a master at spacing the close-set Ortiz eyes and sculpting the fleshy Acosta nose. He had no local equal when it came to sanitizing the reality of a baby wetting its baptismal garments after being sprinkled with holy water; at retouching the internal terror of an otherwise angelic boy in white who had masturbated away his anxiety the night before and was now certain that the holy ghost wafer would refuse to roost in its soiled temple; or at airbrushing the acne from an adolescent with a diploma held out like a magical wand. His specialty, romanticized portraits of graduates, newlyweds and soldiers fresh out of boot camp, was no accident: each breed had no inkling of what it was about to step into.

"Well?" asked his sister Leticia.

He admired the photo on the sly, embarrassed at not doing it justice in the flesh. "Nice. But who is he?"

They exploded in nervous laughter, completely out of proportion to the occasion, as though amazed and relieved that he had returned with a shred of humor.

The men began besieging him with questions, some too trivial to merit more than a nod, others so complex he did not even know where to begin. Several times he tried to leave the company of his uncles and male cousins and edge toward the more intimate circle of women clustered around the dining table. But he found himself politely excluded each time. Even his aunts turned visibly uncomfortable, as though face to face with a paroled ex-convict. "You don't want to talk to us women," said one who shepherded him back to the men. So he returned to the male lair and pretended to enter its drunken camaraderie while the women watched them grow more foolish.

He sat through an awkward, lopsided conversation with his father, who recited the intimate though trivial knowledge every inebriated patriarch felt duty-bound to pass on to his son. Being an only son he had no choice but to pretend to absorb the wisdom; and being the son of a man who idolized war without ever having been there, he wished he could tell him how utterly wrong he was. Finally, in a moment of indecision, while his father paused for another round of cliches, he hinted at his own misgivings. But if his father listened at all, he merely answered with a higher order of platitudes.

"Papa," his older sister Elvia interrupted, "mama needs help moving Tío Plácido."

He offered to assist, but his father insisted he stay. When their father left, Elvia said, "He doesn't want you to see Tío in the condition he's in." He wondered why, since his uncle's benders were almost a family holiday tradition. She must have read his mind. "Tío had promised this time would be different, out of respect for you." She glanced sideways at her husband. "He was fine, until Señor Crudas here started looking for a drinking companion."

"I only pointed him to the eggnog. He dove into the bowl himself."

"You knew perfectly well he would!"

He brought his beer can to his mouth to muffle his reply. "All I know is that I'd rather be dead than a drunk."

"You're making progress on both counts," she said.

He had been home less than three hours and already he felt cheated. Home, or the idea of it, had been nothing more than an imaginary haven, as idealized as the fantasies his Tío Plácido had of it whenever they visited him during his sporadic stays in the veteran's hospital. Home was nothing more than a sanctuary from the assorted metal that screamed through the air or disintegrated beneath your legs and took in your crotch-line by several inches. Home was simply what Nam was not: the lesser evil.

Home was not where God played dice with men's lives like a compulsive gambler with an infinite bankroll. Home was not that custom-made hell that a menopausal nun had invented as a fitting curse for his fourth-grade class trading jungle calls in catechism class, a prophecy he had lived in the flesh in a pre-dawn, psychedelic firefight. "The point," another Chicano survivor of that nightmare had argued, "is to send you back grateful for being alive. After that you'll be America's numbah-one flag-waving vet." So it came down to that: you love the things for which you suffer, a hypothesis the foxhole philosopher had never put to the test. He had met his unmaker in the shape of a Bouncing Betty on a routine patrol, on an otherwise deathly boring afternoon. So then what happened, as in the case of that Fort Worth friend, when the suffering went so far it no longer mattered?

But he was home now; safe, perhaps even sound. But aside from the occasional outbursts of his nieces and nephews, there was little difference between home and Nam. Both here and there the boys drank to push back the terror and the boredom.

"So tell us," his sister Leticia called out, "where were you wounded?"

Even the children turned silent, and he realized his parents had failed to brief the family. "North of Bien Hoa, in a hamlet ... "

"Whoa! That's like saying the moon. I mean what part of you?"

"Now, Leti," said his brother-in-law, "never ask a man about his wounds in love and war."

"In my butt," he said abruptly. And before they could respond he was confessing every absurd detail, down to being evacuated bottoms up on a litter, airlifted while a familiar phrase kept looping through his thoughts: That's how they killed a Japanese. Then he had remembered the first thing he had heard on the Armed Forces radio: Today's Pearl Harbor Day. To add insult to injury he had been dinged with an ancient blunderbuss that could have belonged to Ho Chi Minh's grandfather, so they had zapped his backside once more in case of a rusty musket ball.

He ended his account with a nervous laugh, his first spontaneous reaction since he had come back to the States. But his audience acted more embarrassed than amused, more at home with larger-than-life myths where men walked away from war the better for it, purified of their frailties. He too had once been there, but boot camp had taught him less noble things; arbitrary tyranny, for one.

Yet boot camp, to hear his father's accounts, had been a religious experience, where he had first rubbed elbows with Anglos. The Allies were already mopping up Europe when his father had trained in a kind of gung-ho ghost dance. He had barely shipped out overseas when, as he put it, "Peace broke out." So he had stormed the shores of Italy armed with candy bars and a chronic case of combat interruptus.

His uncle Plácido was the family's real war hero. During the Korean conflict, a Chinese force of near-battalion strength had all but cremated his company, and he had somehow shepherded a handful of other walking wounded for six harrowing days.

But unlike his counterparts from across the tracks, he had been unable to parlay his medals into a secure future. Some blamed his incipient alcoholism, but it had never been clear whether his drinking had been a cause or a consequence of the rejection he had experienced in the hands of the *americanos*. Yet throughout his battle on the home front his brother-in-law Salvador never tired of championing him. Indeed, some suspected that the main reason Salvador Ortiz had married Plácido's youngest sister was to be that much closer to his idol. And except for the sporadic stays at the veterans' hospitals to take the cure, his Tío Plácido had lived with the Ortiz family.

In all that time he had never heard his uncle brag about his bravery. Whenever anyone brought up the topic, his already timid gaze became downright evasive, leading some to suspect that his heroism had been an elaborate mass hoax.

But if his uncle appeared more a dreamer than a doer, there was no mistaking his father's bent. Bellicose when defending his ground, barely on the inertial side of fitness and still a respectable shot despite his dimming eyesight, he seemed an over-the-hill athlete who still harbored the hope that his coach might send him into the game.

"Say," his cousin Jesse said, "the Latin Lovers are playing at the Christmas dance." Four years his junior but already nursing a beer like the rest, Jesse was struggling to keep up with his mentors.

"I saw them play two months ago."

His cousin was impressed. "Zat right? In Nam?"

"That's where I've been. They went to entertain the *raza*."

"Zat right? Well, hell, show up in that uniform here and you can pick just about any *culito* you want."

Their uncle Jorge added, "And you'll be right behind, eh, Jess?"

Jesse's father, whose complex over his coarse features included a certain guilt for having passed them on to his son, stood up. "My Jess doesn't need to pick up leftovers."

His uncle Jorge waved his beer can in mock surrender,

then shifted his axis of interest. "So, *muchacho*, when are we going to win this war?"

He needed no time to think it over. "Soon as the enemy lets us, Tío."

His father walked back in, and his uncle Pepe shouted: "It's not like the Good War, eh, Salvador?"

"Every war's a good war."

"Except for the losers," Leticia added among the laughter.

His father turned serious, as though he had been stone sober all along. "Except for the losers," he agreed quietly.

"What's all this talk about war?" asked his mother. "What kind of Christmas Eve welcome is this for our soldier?"

"Then let's talk about love," said his brother-in-law. "Me, I love beer."

"And barmaids," added his wife.

"But war is as old as love," insisted his father. "Older, even. Why, boys go off to battle before they're men in bed."

"Zat right?" asked Jesse's father.

He knew, without being named, that he had been singled out. This time he weighed his answer carefully. "The only thing war taught me was to hate it."

Suddenly the other men were gulping their beers in silence. His mother stood behind him and soothed his neck. Then, in an ethereal scale that seemed more imagined than sung, she began: "Si-ii-lent night, *noche de paz* . . ."

A few of the children timidly harmonized around her, until his uncle Pepe struggled to his feet. Beer can over his heart, he drowned them out:

"Jo-oo-sé, can you see . . . !" It was a rallying call in reverse, as a dozen distinct monologues broke out, min-

gled with a few off-scale *rancheras*. His mother accepted
her defeat with quiet dignity and went to prepare a snack
for his Tío Plácido. A few minutes later he followed her
into his uncle's bedroom.

She was offering him a cup of Mexican chocolate, taking make-believe sips to stir his appetite. But while his
uncle watched with obvious interest, he seemed oblivious
to her motive.

He followed their stalemate then said, "I have to talk to
you, mama. Alone." He regarded his uncle, whose stare,
unfocused and strabismic, gave him a newborn nature.

"It's all right," she said. "His mind is off God knows
where." Then, before he could marshal his thoughts, she
added, "It's about your going back, isn't it? Don't worry.
The worst is over. Why, before you know it you'll be back
safe—"

"I'm not going back."

She pressed his uncle's hand, making him startle.
"Meaning?"

"Meaning I'm not going back." He took a deep breath,
as though that had only been the prelude. "I don't know
how to tell papa."

"But you're through fighting."

He tried to explain, knowing beforehand he could not.
There was no one overpowering reason, and at the same
time countless minor ones, like the chaotic voices from
the living room, all trying to make themselves heard. "I've
had it. With the whole—"

"I don't understand," she protested.

He knew from experience what she meant to say: I
don't want to understand. "I'll find a way to tell papa
myself."

"He'll die of shame."

He sighed in frustration. Dying of shame was the dis-

ease his kin dreaded most, the way diabetes or congenital
tails haunted other blood lines. "He'll die of shame," she
repeated.

But for him they were mere words, meant to wound
one's pride, and dares such as these had buzzed through
the Nam air, thick but without substance. They had made
a childhood cliche a veritable truism: " ... but words
can never hurt me." Even adolescent boasts had turned
trite: "Death before dishonor." That had made sense until his fifth afternoon in-country, on passing his first enemy corpse sprawled so obscenely that it seemed more
the victim of a gang rape than the hallowed remains of
a hero. And he had realized then and there that nothing
was more dishonorable than death itself. Even now, as he
talked with his mother, he remembered that man more often than his own countrymen did. And it was not shame
that had killed him.

"But you can't just stay here," his mother said.

"I don't plan to."

When the finality of his decision dawned on her, she
became even more lost than he. Suddenly a noise startled
them both, a cross between a cough and a sob. For an
instant he thought it had escaped him unawares.

It was his uncle, eyes watery and burning at the same
time. He made that odd noise again, and suddenly he
recognized the rough outline of his own name. Even his
mother forgot her anguish, or else hid it for his uncle's
sake. "Yes, Plácido! It's him! He's home for Christmas."

Within a matter of seconds his uncle's lucidity seemed
a thing of the past. He tried several times to resuscitate
his uncle's enthusiasm, then finally patted his inert hand.
He was already at the door when his mother called out:
"Please, don't do this to your father." She sounded as
though she herself would end up labeled the deserter, and

it occurred to him that what terrified her most was somehow being held hereditarily accountable for his cowardice. He wished he could reassure her that she had not failed the blood line. The living proof was lying beside her. But in the end he only promised:

"I won't ruin his Christmas."

Encouraged, she pressed on. "Promise you'll reconsider."

He opened the door. "I'll be out of town tomorrow. I need time to think." He walked away, knowing his second statement was a lie.

Christmas Day arrived as advertised: one continuous football feast. By mid-morning his uncles and cousins were already sprawled around the living room set warming up with pageants and previews. Twice he tried to enter the he-man circle of hyperbole only to feel his face contort this way or that. Finally the gladiators on the screen came out in their neat, snug uniforms that threw their muscles in relief, and the colorcasters gushed on like lovesick adolescents camouflaging their crushes with manly metaphors of war: offensive drives, holding the line, field generals, blitzes. It stood to reason. The messier the real front became, the more the folks back home needed their twentieth-century cowboys in tailored, Lone Ranger uniforms, winning decisively and by the clock. And even fighting away from home, the worst they could expect from alien turf was its being artificial.

His nephews were comparing last night's booty. Children had their Santa Claus, and adults were entitled to something similar, even if he turned out to be John Wayne swaggering in buckskins and coon cap one year, beret and tiger leotards the next. The enemy had its Uncle Ho, our side its Saint Ho-ho-ho. Two sides of the same coin.

His youngest nephew was leafing through a coloring

book and improvising a story-line as he went along. He remembered his own boyhood comics, with Superman saving a miniature world of his childhood and preserving it under a glass dome. "*Qué padre*," he used to think, "to grow up and keep your past intact and timeless." You would not even need to return. Simply knowing that you could was enough.

"Your Tío Plácido wants to give you his blessing now," said his mother. "In case he doesn't see you again."

"Every time that man has a hangover," said his uncle Jorge, "he's ready to check out of this world."

His father glanced at the packed duffel bag by the bedroom door. "Eager to get back so soon, son?"

"I'm helping Santa with late deliveries."

His mother covered for him. "He's visiting friends in Falfurrias. They're here for three days." She turned to her brother-in-law. "As for my brother, he's feeling better, no thanks to you. He was going through his box of war mementos this morning."

But the moment his uncle entered the room he laid to rest any hopes of a quick recovery. Braced by the walking cane he used as a last resort, he seemed to stand at death's door, with that unique agony of alcoholics torn between a brutal hangover and the tortuous prospect of satiating it. Even at that distance he emanated the sour breath of convalescence. He uttered something in that unsteady voice that suddenly leapt from a bleat to a shout startling even him, as though a mouse had roared.

Fortunately his mother interpreted: "He wants you to come closer for his blessing."

He knelt while his uncle went on in that unintelligible litany that gave the ceremony a pagan ring. Several times he felt the staff brush his shoulders as if he were being knighted and chastised at once. Then his mother said,

"He wants to give you an *abrazo*."

He stood and returned the farewell hug, and felt the full weight of his uncle trying so desperately to articulate but growing more frustrated with each futile attempt. "Yes, Tío," he pacified him without the least insight into his ravings, "yes, I understand." Finally his uncle began tugging at him violently, almost tearing at his jacket, until his mother made a swift gesture to the others to pull them apart. He started to protest that his uncle was not hurting him when the two Jesses yanked back the clinging invalid with such force that it seemed they were breaking up a fight.

He returned to his bedroom to pack his last belongings and prepare his so-longs, when he felt something protruding from his jacket pocket. He pulled it out, more mystified than curious.

It was an old letter in Spanish, dated before his birth and addressed to his Tío Plácido. He paused to admire the manicured calligraphy, each longhand letter so stylized yet so personal that he could not help but wonder whether whoever had penned it were still alive.

The author, who referred to his Tío Plácido as her cousin, made reference to earlier correspondence, asking him whether enlisting in the war to stay in the United States and facilitate his citizenship was worth the price. "I shall respect your decision, but my offer of sanctuary, if you so choose, remains." She ended on a prophetic note: "Now you must choose: a hero, or a happy man." Her words sounded dated, distant, yet they echoed his own conscience and his own concerns. Their "offer of sanctuary," suggesting a long-ago peace of mind, calmed his own thoughts.

He examined the envelope and noted the last line of the return address that his Tío Plácido had circled recently and laboriously. And suddenly the strained, garbled message as urgent as if his uncle's own life depended on it, became clear: "México! México!"

# Frontier

Don Benito Leal was still on his first cup of coffee at the Early Bird Cafe when a bus boy cleaning up a window booth glanced outside. "Someone wants you, judge." He nodded toward his office.

"Already? Who?"

"Can't tell from here. But they've got a pickup truck I'd give my left leg for."

Don Benito was debating whether to take a look when the cafe owner came over and poured him another cup. "Let them wait, don Benito. Your son let them in already. Besides, you're the judge."

He did nothing to acknowledge the remark, for he was not one to fall for flattery or the small trappings of his office. As justice of the peace his everyday duties revolved around setting bails, settling small claims and assessing traffic fines. He was not, he would often insist, a "real" judge.

But it was useless to protest the honor. His predecessor, his own father, had long since retired, but he was still known as *señor juez*.

Don Benito felt just as uncomfortable over being called

43

"don". Although it added an aura of respect, the title also added years to a man already balding before his time.

He took the owner's advice and savored his second cup of coffee. All at once he remembered that along with the car keys he had given his son money to buy anti-acid tablets on his way to the office. He patted his back pocket where his wallet was not, and had a small panic at finding himself penniless.

He tried to make his search as guarded as possible, but a moment later he heard: "No problem, *señor juez*. It's on the house."

The thought that a free cup of coffee might one day end up tipping the scales of justice on the owner's behalf made him dig into his front pockets, where he pulled out a crumpled bill. "This should cover it," he said. "Including a tip."

Outside, he greeted the few faces he knew by name. The rest, all recent immigrants, had the daily familiarity of strangers that one saw on the street, but beyond that their identities were a blur. Two or three even looked away, the give-away tic of the undocumented passer-by.

At times he wished he could put them at ease, explaining that he had no intention of turning them in, any more than he would the restaurant's undocumented cooks. But some unspoken etiquette always discouraged him, because then they would know that he knew. And once that happened, he was publicly a party to their illegality.

It's better this way, he told himself—playing hide-and-go-seek in the open.

He had grown up in this border town and had come to know it well. But today, taking his morning walk to his office, he felt the uneasiness of the outsider. He could count at least one business serving as a front for laundered drug money: Morales' Pickup Paradise, where he noticed a young Mexican prostitute who had already crossed the border by bus that morning.

The early bird catches the worm, he thought. It certainly seemed true in this case. She was perched atop a four-wheel drive truck, talking to none other than the owner.

Don Benito softened his steps, hoping to surprise and shame Joe Morales, who had his back to him. But when Joe pulled out his wallet in full view of every passer-by, it was don Benito who was taken aback. Seeing him, the girl suddenly jumped off the hood and pretended to examine the truck.

Joe kept the judge at bay with an uneasy grin while he invented an alibi. "Morning, don Benny. I was just serenading this young lady into buying a pickup."

Don Benito kept his gaze on Joe's hands. "I always heard you gave the best deals in town, Joe. Now you even pay clients to drive them off the lot?"

Joe did a minor sleight of hand. "Every customer gets a card."

Don Benito answered in English to keep the girl in the dark: "Isn't she a bit young to get behind the wheel?"

"It's the new generation, judge. They're driving before they can walk."

"Plus a lot of other things." He glanced at the girl, then at Joe, and added in Spanish: "I suppose it's never too early to take care of business."

"I was just about to say the same thing of you, don Benny."

Don Benito squinted toward his office while Joe Morales tilted his sunglasses for a better look. "Don Roque's truck, judge. Too bad he's not downwind. Then I could've guessed with my eyes closed."

Don Benito felt somewhat relieved that the visit did

not involve drugs. "Sure it's his?"

"If you're asking me to swear on a stack of Bibles I'd have to say it's his son's. But don Roque personally bought it from this lot. See that decal with the pig in profile? They added that later. Sort of ruins the whole effect, don't you think?"

"You know what they say about beauty, Joe."

"And you know what they say about don Roque. He only has eyes for his pigs. And the man likes his females in pigtails too."

Joe puffed his gestures in imitation of don Roque's airs, frequent in self-made men. Then his hand shot out so decisively that don Benito extended his own without thinking. Joe then sounded out don Roque's way of presenting himself. "The sausage king at your service. And I mean the real kind. Pork."

Joe was a superb mimic, and don Benito laughed, certain that Joe did not spare him behind his back.

"Correct me if I'm wrong, don Benny. They say he picks up the stray mutts that are dumped outside the city limits, then adds them to his *chorizo*. He does the same with coyotes shot in his ranch."

"I don't eat sausage. And I've never tasted coyote. So I wouldn't know, Joe." Don Benito was sure that whatever he said in confidence, Joe would exaggerate and repeat all day.

He was still chuckling when Joe said, "It's good to know you haven't lost your sense of humor. With elections almost here, I mean."

Don Benito merely blinked his eyes. Joe continued with his jokes, and the judge furrowed his eyebrows. "You mean you didn't know, don Benny? It's all over town. This time around you have an opponent."

For a long while, don Benito simply smiled at Joe.

Then he realized Joe was serious. "An opponent," he said. He repeated it in a low, flat tone. "An opponent."

Joe Morales grasped the judge's shoulder."You know you have my vote, don Benny."

The abrupt pledge, coming from nowhere, surprised him, and it took him a while to see the hollowness of the gesture: a convicted felon, Joe Morales could not vote.

"I'll go a step further, don Benny. Send me bumper stickers, and I'll put them on every bumper on my lot." He patted the girl's behind. "Even the ones with wide loads."

The thought of free advertising was tempting for don Benito, but the idea of his name next to Joe's advertising plates kept him from responding to the offer.

"What do you say, don Benny?"

He had trouble coming up with a reply, partly because he did not wish to offend Joe, but mostly because his mind was still on his mystery opponent. Finally he managed:

"Do you know what a poor politician is, Joe?"

"Is this a riddle?"

"It's a sad fact of life, friend. It means I can't afford stickers."

"How much do you need?" Joe reached for his wallet with the same flourish he had shown earlier as he tried to impress the prostitute.

Don Benito shook his head and left him with a parting lesson. "I'm afraid you can't buy justice, Joe."

Joe Morales, determined to have the last word, squeezed the girl to his side. "Who wants to buy her? I just need to rent her, that's all."

Don Benito followed the front row of new pick-ups facing the street. Several had license plates that read "Texas Dealer". He tried to savor the irony but could not get past the beginnings of heartburn.

As soon as he crossed the street he made out the logo
on don Roque's truck—a crowned hog, with a radiant halo
in the background. He breathed another sigh of relief that
his first visitors were not pushers or pimps. But beneath
the gratitude he remained ill at ease, as if his heartburn
had degenerated into a metaphysical symptom. Blaming
it on don Roque's sign was not enough. The very core of
the man discomforted don Benito.

Rumor had it that don Roque's wife had wasted away
because he had refused to take her to a doctor. Instead
he had subjected her to homemade remedies until the day
she died.

That had been almost two decades ago. But don Benito
still remembered clearly an anonymous voice in the middle of the night, calling out to his father from their front
yard. "Don Diógenes! *Señor juez!* Roque's father-in-
law just left the *cantina.* He's been there since the burial
this morning. Now he says he's going to turn Roque into
*chorizo* with his .410!"

The old judge boarded his station wagon armed with
nothing more than a flashlight. But Benito, who had insisted on going with him, literally rode shotgun, slipping
a twelve gauge under the seat.

The flashlight in fact proved more useful. They found
the father-in-law in one of Roque's pigpens, sobbing in-
consolably, surrounded by spent shells and gut-shot hogs.
A few survivors scrambled in panic among the carnage.

Don Benito still remembered the hogs' squeals, both
terrified and terrifying, and their frenzied stampede. He
still believed what he had learned back then—that Christ
surely must have cast a madman's demons into swine.

To this day, don Benito could neither forget the scene
nor forgive the old man. Don Roque, though, had never
grieved, nor did he harbor the slightest remorse. It was

even rumored that the night of the shooting he had been at his mistress' shack, "being consoled". As for his wife, she had given him six sons, and probably would have given him a full dozen had she not died.

She was long since dead, thought don Benito as he approached his office. Don Roque, on the other hand, gave every impression he would live to greet the next generation.

The lipstick-red pickup was parked alongside his own car, a sedan so nondescript that every teenager in the barrio, including his own son, called it 'The Narcmobile.' He thought he glimpsed a young woman behind the window, but the immobile profile made him wonder whether he had imagined her.

Don Benito's son was trying his best to tidy up the office under the amused eyes of both don Roque and his own son. Both watched don Benito's son in wonder.

Don Roque greeted the judge in with the hale and hearty voice of someone more at home in open spaces: "Don Benito, send your boy to my ranch some day to help us clean house."

"This is his weekend job."

"All the more reason. We have the worst luck keeping maids worth a damn."

Cursed with his mother's compulsive touch, the boy continued moving a pile of books from some chairs to a bookcase. Don Roque's son, several years older and with a farmer's physique, offered to help but receiving no encouragement, he made a helpless gesture and told his father, "I wouldn't even know where all those books go."

Don Roque also surveyed the bookshelf in wonder, amazed that people could have so much to scribble about. Then, because he could not explain the phenomenon any other way, he told his son, "I'll bet those books go back to when don Benito's own father was judge. Am I right, *señor juez?*"

Since he saw no harm in humoring him, don Benito ran his hand along a row of book spines and drew one out. "Between these covers you'll find every soul born in this barrio." He pulled out a second tome at random. "And here you'll find those who departed for the next one ... "

Don Roque jabbed his son in the ribs. "That's God's truth! His father married your mother and me. Hell, I'll bet our crosses are buried somewhere in there."

Don Benito suddenly realized that the white lie might snowball into a small bureaucratic avalanche, so he side-tracked the conversation.

"Did I see a girl inside your truck, or did I imagine her?"

"A little filly, *verdad?*"

"I couldn't tell ... "

"If I were ten years younger I'd saddle and mount her myself."

The judge let don Roque continue, since there was no stopping him. Besides he enjoyed listening, even though afterwards he felt something like a slight moral hangover. Don Roque had an earthy, barnyard humor that bordered on cruelty. Don Benito had learned from experience that there were men in this world who lacked both outright malice as well as an ounce of compassion, and don Roque numbered among them. Sometimes he felt that was the best way to live.

Don Roque, as if suddenly realizing he had hogged the conversation, said, "So how are you feeling, *señor juez?*"

"Aside from a little heartburn ... " He soothed his chest to hold down an eruption. Don Roque gave a know-ing grunt, and don Benito already knew his remedy:

"The black potion! Hell, it'll kill anything from crabs to cancer."

Don Benito felt another wave of indigestion, and for an instant he thought he might blurt out, "I heard it killed your wife." Instead he gulped down the sourness. "The black potion. My grandfather used to swear by it."

"And look how long he lived."

Don Benito made another sound like a suppressed hiccup. "Excuse me, gentlemen."

"I'll bet you're eating beef sausage," said don Roque.

"Actually, I don't prefer any ... "

"Beef *chorizo* does that to people. That's what they get for messing with nature. Now, my boy here thinks I'm crazy, but I say that's why we're getting these new, strange diseases." All at once he turned quiet, as though absorbed in a deep, philosophical mystery, and stared at a row of books for clues. "Tell me ... What on earth would possess a man to prefer beef *chorizo*?"

"These days people are more careful with their health." Don Benito's answer came at a mindless moment, and he realized at once that it made as much sense as don Roque's question. Sausage was sausage. You couldn't change that fact any more than you could alter the proverbial sow's ear.

But the asinine remark had not fallen on deaf ears. Don Roque's entrepreneurial head went to work right away. "If I could only corral the crowd that eats weeds, *señor juez*. Everyone talks about being 'healthy as an ox', but whoever gives credit to pigs? Hell, they'll survive anywhere."

The judge, hoping that the visitors would give attention to the matter at hand, grabbed a book at random and pretended to consult a point of law in his best judicial pose. But don Roque simply turned to the judge's son in hushed admiration. "Your father's a very smart man."

Raised in the company of books, the boy only shrugged.

Don Roque cleared his throat. "Well, even an idiot like me knows elections are almost here."

The judge smiled wanly. "Joe Morales just reminded me."

"That Joe Morales." He copied don Benito's smile, shook his head and stared at the floor. Then, still shaking his head, he glanced up and frowned. "Watch out for him, don Benito. The man's a backstabber."

Don Roque's son nodded. "That he is." Then he caught the puzzled look on the judge's face. "You know he's backing your opponent."

Don Benito felt the dread of a dream about to collapse into a nightmare. For an instant he imagined himself an over-the-hill boxer in his corner, about to face an unknown opponent.

"You mean you didn't know?," don Roque asked. "They're waiting till the last minute to file. That's how these people operate, *señor juez*. Dirty and lowdown."

"Papa says our pigs could teach them a few manners."

"Politics isn't pretty," said don Benito. It was a phrase whose bitter pragmatism he had never had to taste personally, and whose wisdom he had not appreciated until now, when he found himself on the receiving end of the advice.

"You need us," said don Roque. "The salt of the earth. Decent, hard-working people. Take away my money and land and I'm just a pig farmer. But I'm a lot cleaner than that scum down the street. That's why we need you as judge, don Benito. And you need us. Hell, if I could I'd train my pigs to trot right into that voting booth, close that little curtain and pull the lever."

Don Benito found the thought downright insulting but did not say so. Instead he said, "I'm afraid they'd end up voting for my opponent. Anyway, if I need them I'll let you know."

"It'll be here sooner than you think, *señor juez*. At my age you'd think time would slow down, just so I could keep up."

Don Benito clicked his ballpoint pen several times. "Time waits for no man."

"Well, sir," said don Roque, taking the hint, "we won't keep you waiting."

But they did, and they remained mute until the judge acted on a hunch:

"This involves the girl in the truck?"

Don Roque's son looked first at his father, then at don Benito, and nodded.

The judge ventured a second, more intimate, guess. "You two are getting married?"

"Oh, no, don Benito! That's Perla out there! Our maid!"

The judge, hoping to salvage his wisdom in their eyes, guessed again. "She's pregnant?"

"No, sir, not at all! In fact that's why ... "

"In fact, coming here was her idea. She said if we didn't bring her over she'd get here herself."

"She's an illegal, don Benito. I tell you, those outside the law are always the first to cry foul."

Don Roque saw the potential trap in his son's comments. "Now, son, we don't know if she's here crooked or not. All we know is her Spanish sounds too good for these parts." Saying that, don Roque edged toward the door and peered out. She must have seen him, for the pickup door on the passenger's side opened at once.

Like the girl don Benito had seen earlier, she appeared much younger than he had expected. But her slow, painful walk seemed out of sorts with her youth.

The instant she entered the office, her burning eyes told him she had called on all her courage to take those steps. Looking at her, he felt an empathy for the underdog that political cynicism had almost asphyxiated.

Don Roque must have caught the concern, for he put a word in edgewise. "At first I felt sorry for her. A man tries to do what's right, but nowadays no one's worth the sacrifice."

He turned and stared at the girl, waiting for her to lose her nerve. She held her ground, but neither did she dispute him.

Don Benito cleared his throat and managed a paternal tone. "Now, *señorita*, how can I help?"

"*Señor juez*," she began. "It's about don Roque's son ... " She stopped and stared at don Benito's own boy until he scratched a pimple on his chin.

"Don't be embarrassed, *señorita*. He's heard almost everything there is to hear." Don Benito added with a touch of pride, "He's even assisted me in pronouncing deaths."

When she still said nothing, the boy put on the headphones hanging from his neck and clicked on the portable tape player clipped to his belt. Once he started nodding to the music, she said: "Don Roque's son had his way with me."

Don Roque's son protested, but the judge motioned him still. "And where did this happen, *señorita*?"

"At their house. I'm their maid."

"She's also a wetback," said the son. "Twice! From some country I never even heard of." He looked at her and smiled, satisfied that his revenge had thwarted her case.

Don Benito covered his eyes as the last glimmer of justice seemed to dim from the world. His faintness swelled into a hollow impotence, and he grabbed a book at random, a tome on property rights, pretending to consult a point of law.

Don Roque's son whispered loudly: "You shouldn't even be here. You're breaking the law!"

The judge raised his voice while keeping his eyes lowered. "So are you, for having hired her."

"Now, *señor juez*," said don Roque. "Like I said, we don't know how she got here, and we don't care. We took her on out of pity more than anything else. And now she bites the hand that fed her."

Don Benito said nothing, doodling on a pad and scratching where his scalp already showed. He did not need to explain how difficult it was to help aliens with visas, much less illegals. Finally, as a last resort, he asked, "Are you pregnant, *señorita*?"

"Oh, no, *señor*!"

As if to show that there went her last hope, he swiveled his chair, shifting his axis away from her.

The girl stood up out of desperation. "That's why I'm ... " She glanced at don Benito's boy again, then walked around the desk and told her story in urgent whispers.

Don Benito sat and listened, almost immobile. Only the knuckles on his right hand blanched as he clenched a lead glass paper weight.

Finally she stepped back. "Judge for yourself, *señor juez*! That's why I can barely walk, much less work."

Don Benito tried to talk but instead gagged on his outrage. He stared at don Roque's son until he became coherent. "Is it true? What she said you did to her?"

Don Benito stood up suddenly; when the casters on his chair jammed, he pushed it hard against the far wall. It almost collided against don Roque's son, and the judge cornered him as he moved out of the way. "What's wrong

with you, hombre?! Or am I talking to the wrong species?
You're not an animal, are you?"

"No, *señor juez*, but ... "

"But what?! You live a civilized society, don't you?
Not in some cave."

"Yes, *señor juez* ... " He stared at his own father, but
don Roque seemed just as terrified. Even the girl pro-
tected herself with crossed arms.

"Then how could you do such a thing?! You might
have ruined her for life!"

"It was her idea."

Don Benito glared at him, but when the young man
held his stare the judge turned to the girl. "Is he telling
the truth?"

Her pause encouraged her accuser. "It was her idea,"
he repeated. "O.K., maybe I was a little rough and messed
her up a bit. Hell, how should I know?"

Don Benito still stared at the girl. "Is it true?"

"I couldn't fight him off, *señor juez*. And I couldn't
risk getting pregnant either. So I ... " She approached the
judge to talk to him in private once more, but don Benito
backed away like a man betrayed. Feeling nauseous, he
motioned his son to remove his earphones then told him
to bring his heartburn medicine from the car. Then he
swept a hand at the three in front of him and said in a
weak voice, "Get out."

"You mean her?" said don Roque's son.

"All of you."

At first his silence only glued them to the spot, as
though they feared a trick or a test of some sort. Then
don Benito's son showed them the door. "He'll be all
right. It's just his indigestion."

The girl was the first to leave. She went to the pickup,
opened the door, took her purse and walked away.

Don Roque nudged his son and whispered, "Let's go. We got what we came for."

Alone, don Benito slowly drew strength from the silence. At length he shuffled to the window, parted the blinds and gazed out at the daily activity with the exhausted look of a convalescent.

A car stopped at the corner of the cafe. A transvestite in a summer dress let himself out and waited for his next customer.

Don Benito's son, returning from the car, paused to watch with fascination. When he saw his father spying on both of them, he hurried into the office.

Don Benito, though, continued looking out the window.

"Are you all right, papa?"

He nodded, but his thoughts seemed elsewhere. "I remember when I was your age. Back then there was no Joe Morales pickup lot. The Early Bird was the Chulas Fronteras Cafe. After school we'd get together ... This used to be such a nice barrio. Now it's another Sodom."

"It's not all that bad, papa. At least it's never dull."

His son's faint praise did little to cheer his spirits. After a while he said, almost to himself, "So what will become of her?"

"The girl who was here? You haven't seen the last of her, papa. Next year she'll be out on the street."

"Maybe by then so will I."

"Don't worry. The good guys always come to the rescue."

"I think this time they ran out the door."

He took his medication and sat behind the desk. Then he folded his arms, shut his eyes and waited for the medicine to do its job.

# Too Much His Father's Son

In the middle of the argument, without warning, Arturo's mother confronted her husband point-blank: "Is it another woman?»

"For heaven's sake, Carmela, not in front of—"

"Nine is old enough to know. You owe both of us that much."

Sitting in the room, Arturo could not help but overhear. Usually he could dissimulate with little effort—being a constant chaperone on his cousin Anita's dates had made him a master at fading into the background. But at that moment he was struggling hard to control a discomfort even more trying than those his cousin and her boy friends put him through.

The argument had already lasted an hour and, emotionally, his mother had carried its brunt. Trying to keep her voice in check was taking more out of her than if she had simply vented her tension.

His father, though, lay fully clothed in bed, shirt half-buttoned and hands locked under his head. From his closed eyes and placid breathing, one would have thought that her frustration was simply lulling him into a more

profound relaxation. Only an occasional gleam from those
perfect, white teeth told Arturo he was still listening, and
even then with bemused detachment.

"Is it another woman, Raúl?"

His father batted open his eyes only to look away, as
though the accusation did not even merit the dignity of a
defense. His gaze caught Arturo and tried to lock him into
the masculine intimacy they often shared, an unspoken
complicity between father and son. But at that instant it
simply aggravated Arturo's shame.

"Who is she, Raúl?"

His smile made it clear that if there were another
woman, he was not saying. "You tell me. You're the one
who made her up."

Arturo had seen that smile in all its shadings—
sometimes with disarming candor, but more often full of
arrogance. When his father wished, his smile could become a gift of pearls, invigorating all who saw his teeth
shining with their special luster.

Yet at other times his father needed only to curl his
lips, and those same teeth turned into a sadistic show of
strength. Well aware of his power over others, the father
seemed indifferent as to whether the end effect exalted or
belittled.

Out of nowhere, perhaps to add to the confusion, he
ordered, "Bring *abuelo*'s belt, Arturo."

Instead of strapping it on, he pretended to admire what
had once been his own father's gun belt. The holster
was gone, but a bullet that had remained rusted inside a
middle clasp added a certain authority. The hand-tooled
leather, a rich dark brown, had delicate etchings now too
smooth to decipher. His grandfather Edelmiro had been a
large, mean-looking man in life, and Arturo still remembered the day his father received the belt. He had strapped

it on for only a moment, over his own belt. Later that day Arturo opened the closet for a closer inspection and had come upon his father, piercing another notch for his smaller waist.

His mother continued to confront his father, who idly looped the belt, grabbed it at opposite ends and began whapping it with a solemn force. At first the rhythmic slaps disconcerted her, until she turned their tension into punctuations for her own argument. Suddenly the belt cracked so violently that Arturo thought the ancient cartridge had fired. He was startled, as much from the noise as from the discovery that his father's legendary control had snapped. For an instant both parents, suddenly realizing how far things had gone, appeared paralyzed.

No, his father would never strike her, he was sure of that. But nobody had ever pushed him that far, least of all his mother, whose own strength had always been her patience.

He wondered why his eyes were suddenly brimming. Perhaps trespassing into the unknown terrified him, or perhaps he was ashamed of his father's indifference. That confusion—crying without knowing why—frightened him even more.

"See, Carmela? Now you've got the boy blubbering."

He was hoping to hide his weakness from his father, and the unmasking only added to the disgrace. Desperate to save face, he yelled, "I'm leaving!"

As always his father turned the threat in his favor. "That's good, son. Wait outside and let me handle this."

"I'm going to *papá grande*'s house!"

Arturo had never been that close to his mother's family, and that made his decision all the more surprising. But if his father felt betrayed he did not show it. "Fine, then. You're on your own."

It took him a while to catch his father's sarcasm and his own unthinking blunder: he did not know the way to his grandparents' house. He had walked there only once—last Sunday—and that time his mother had disoriented him with a different route from the one his father took.

But now, standing there facing his father, he had no choice. Rushing out the kitchen door he ran across the back yard, expecting at any moment to be stopped in his tracks. When his arms brushed against a clothesline, he almost tripped as if his father had lassoed him with his belt. Not until he reached the alley did he realize he had been hoping his father would indeed stop him, even with a word.

He crossed the alley into an abandoned lot. There he matted a patch of grass and weeds reaching his waist and settled in, so as to give his heart time to hush. He sat for a long time, wondering whether to gather his thoughts or let them scramble until nothing mattered.

From doña Chole's house came the blare of a Mexican radio station. Two announcers were sandwiching every song with a frenzied assault. Farther away David's father continued working on his pet project—a coop and flypen for his game cocks: four or five swift whacks into wood ... silence ... then another volley. For a while he lost himself in the hammering. If he listened closer he could hear the cursing and singing that gave the neighborhood life. Only his own home remained absolutely still.

Soon the sun began to get in his eyes whenever he looked homeward. A cool breeze was blowing at his back, and if he waited in the weeds a sun-toasted aroma penetrated his corduroy shirt.

Someone was coming up the path, making soft lashing sounds in the weeds. His intuition told him that the person was Fela the *curandera* and when he finally dared peek he immediately dove back into his hiding place, wondering whether to congratulate or curse himself.

A part of him scrambled for a rational explanation: who else could it be? Fela the healer was the only grown-up unconcerned about snakes in the undergrowth. In her daily forages for herbs she was used to cutting swaths through the weeds. Yet another side of him was forced to side with the barrio lore—that she had special powers, that she appeared and disappeared at will, that she could think your thoughts before they occurred to you.

The brushing got closer, so he lay very still, trying to imitate his father's self-discipline. When the rustling suddenly stopped, he swore the waft of his corduroy shirt had given him away.

A voice called out: "Since when do little boys live in the wild?"

His heart began beating wildly, but her tone carried enough teasing that he half-raised his head.

"You're hiding from someone?"

All at once, he had a clear image of his father sprawled across the bed, amused, almost bored. Arturo answered her question with a nod, afraid that if he spoke, his rage might leap out and injure them both.

"You did something bad?"

He managed a hoarse, determined vow: "I'm going to smash my father's teeth."

He expected the violence in his words to stun her, but instead she disarmed him with a kind smile. "Whatever for? He has such nice teeth. Some day yours will look just like his."

For a moment, in place of the familiar habit of his own body, he experienced an undefined numbness, followed by the fascinated terror of someone who has inherited a gleaming crown with awesome responsibilities. He stood speechless, repulsed yet tempted by the thought of turning into his father.

"Anyway," she added, "before you know it he'll be old and toothless like me."

She picked a row of burrs clinging to her faded dress, then said as she left, "And tell your mother she's in my thoughts and prayers." Watching her walk away, he tried without success to retrace the route he and his mother had taken to her father's house at the time of their secret visit last Sunday.

That Sunday morning, while his mother talked to Fela in the living room, he had sat on a wicker chair in Fela's porch, entertained by Cuco, an ancient caged parrot with colorful semi-circles under his eyes. Arturo was feeding him chile from a nearby plant to make him talk. "Say it," he urged between bribes: "*Chinga tu madre*"—. But the chile only agitated Cuco's whistling.

"Come on, you stupid bird. *Chinga tu madre.* Screw your mother."

Suddenly there was a raucous squawk. "Screw your *padre* instead!"

As he wheeled about and felt the blood rush to his face, Fela was already raising her arms in innocence. "Who says he's stupid? That's an exotic, bilingual bird you're talking to."

From there, he and his mother had gone to his grand-parents' house. Her route through alleys and unfenced backyards led him to ask, "How do you know all these shortcuts?"

She had paused to dry her forehead on her sleeve, and for the first time in days he had seen her smile. "I grew up in this barrio. This is where I used to play."

Trying to imagine her at the same age he now was, he had to smile to himself.

When they got to his grandfather's house, they had to wait until his grandfather Marcelo finished his *radionovela*. Then, after hearing where they had been and why, his grandfather shook his head. "I knew your marriage would come to this. But going to Fela was a mistake. If he finds out he'll claim you're trying to win him back through witchcraft."

"I had to know if he's seeing another woman."

"And what if he is?"

Arturo had never seen her as serene and as serious as when she answered, "Then he's not worth winning back."

"But a *curandera* ... Why not see a priest?"

Arturo's grandmother took her side. "What for, Marcelo? He'd only give her your advice: accept him as your cross in life."

"I wouldn't in this case. An unfaithful husband is one thing, an arrogant s.o.b. is another. Still, a priest could say a few prayers in your behalf."

"Fela offered to do that herself."

"And no doubt offered good advice," his grandmother added.

His mother's fist clenched his own. "Yes," she said, and her firmness made it obvious that was the last word.

His grandfather, deep in thought, held his breath without taking his eyes off him. Then he closed them and exhaled a stale rush of cigarette smoke, as if unclouding his thoughts. "I've always said your father was a *cabrón*."

"Now, Marcelo. Don't turn him against his own father," his grandmother interjected.

"Mamá's right. None of this is Arturo's fault. He's going through enough as it is."

"True. But I still wouldn't give a kilo of crap for the whole de la O family, starting with Edelmiro."

"May he rest in peace," said his grandmother.

His grandfather stood up. "Not if there's a devil down below."

"Marcelo! He was your *compadre.*"

"I had as much choice in the matter as the boy had in being his grandson." He turned to Arturo's mother. "Remember, if there's a falling out, don't ask that family for anything. Your place is here."

His grandmother added, "And of course that includes Arturo. He's as much a part of the family as the rest of us."

His grandfather had simply said, "Let's hope he's not too much his father's son."

By now the late afternoon sun was slanting long, slender shadows his way, but he was determined to spend the night there if need be. He began counting in cycles of hundreds to keep his uncertainty in check.

Suddenly the rear screen door opened and his father leaned against it, his belt slung over his chest and shoulder like a bandoliered and battle-weary warrior.

"Arturo, come inside." Whenever he wanted to conceal something from the neighbors, he used that phrase.

Arturo slowly stood up but held his ground, as much from stubbornness as dread.

"It's all right, son." His father sounded final yet forgiving, like a king who had put down a castle uprising, regained control, and had decided to pardon the traitors.

Arturo blinked but once, but his pounding heart made even something that small seem a life-and-death concession.

Then his mother appeared alongside his father, and for an instant, framed by the doorway, their pose reminded him of their newlywed portrait in the living room: his hands at his sides, her own clasped in front, both heads slightly tilted as if about to rest on each other's shoulder.

In that eye blink of an interval before she stepped outside, he felt like an outsider looking in.

She was halfway between him and the house when his father said, "Your mother's bringing you back."

He could not believe her betrayal. After all that, she had surrendered and was bringing him in as well. He wanted to cry out at her for having put him through so much. But another part of him understood he shared the blame, for not helping her, for being too much his father's son.

"I forgot the way," he said. Although she was quite close he could not tell whether she heard—much less accepted—his timid apology. He managed his first step homeward when she blocked his path, gently took his hand and guided him in the opposite direction.

He heard, or perhaps only imagined, his father: "Come back." He tugged her arm in case she had not heard. She tightened her grasp to show that she had. Then, intuiting his dilemma, she paused, saying nothing but still gazing away from the house. He realized then and there that the decision was for him alone to make. Hers had already been made.

Unable to walk back or away, he felt like the only living thing in the open. Then his father called out, "Son," and he knew it was his last call. His spine shivered as though a weapon had been sighted at his back, and he imagined his father removing from his belt the cartridge reserved for the family traitor.

There was no way of telling how long he braced himself for whatever was coming, until he finally realized that the moment of reckoning was already behind him. It was then that he felt his father's defeat in his own blood. With it came the glorious fear of a fugitive burning his bridges into the unknown, or a believer orphaned from a false faith.

And in that all-or-nothing instant that took so little doing and needed even less understanding, his all-powerful
father evaporated into the myth he had always been.

He felt a flesh-and-blood grasp that both offered and
drew strength. He began to walk away, knowing there was
no turning back.

# Old Acquaintances

In a matter of hours the new year would arrive. But Elena, a sophomore majoring in sociology, still owed on the old one. She had spent most of the day in the university library, working on a term paper for a class in which she had taken an incomplete.

The library closed early in preparation for the holiday, and Elena found herself anxious but with nothing to do. All at once she remembered that her friend Sylvia would be getting out early from work.

She found her in the front yard, covering her plants.

"It hasn't been that cold so far," said Elena.

"You never know."

Sylvia walked up and tapped the car roof. "How's Dolores?"

"With any luck she'll make it to the new year. After that, all bets are off."

Sylvia glanced at the textbooks in the backseat. "I thought the semester was over."

"It's an old course." Elena smiled at the irony. "I'm specializing in gerontology."

"In what?"

"We study old people."

Sylvia stifled a yawn, something she did whenever Elena mentioned school. "Old people are history."

"Well, right now they're my future. Besides, we'll all get there some day."

Sylvia, several years older than her friend, said, "Don't remind me."

"Anyway, now I have to interview ten elderly people. Half Anglos, half Hispanics."

"Our people shouldn't be a problem." She swept her hand as though they were lined along the horizon. "But good luck with the gringos."

"They're around."

"But what makes you think they'll talk to you?"

"Times have changed, Sylvia."

"Not for old Anglos. For them time stands still."

Elena reshuffled her papers. "Well, it's not standing still for me. I have to find ten respondents, and from the same vicinity."

"We're back to where we started, then. Anglos are around, all right, but not around here." Sylvia swept her hand once more. "You want white faces, you go to the north side of town."

Elena hated to admit it, but her friend was right. She was about to concede the point when the thought occurred to her:

"So who said it had to be in the city?" She answered Sylvia's blank stare. "Drive outside the city limits and what do you see?"

"*Colonias.* Barrios."

"And right next to them?"

Sylvia thought a moment. "Trailer parks for Anglo snowbirds."

Elena corrected her. "Winter Texans. I don't think they like the term snowbirds."

Sylvia was undaunted. "And I don't like the term Mexican girl. But that's what they call me at the store."

This time Elena did not even argue the point. "Whatever. What do you say we scout the territory?"

"We'd better hurry, then. It's already five."

Elena knew that her friend never wore a watch after work, and her own was at home, waiting to be repaired. "How do you know the time?"

"Don Vicente's waiting for the bus." Sylvia pointed to the old man standing at the opposite corner. "For the last three months he's been taking that trip like clockwork. Then again, what else would you expect from a watch repairman?"

"Who would have thought?" Elena's voice trailed as she stared at the right hand he usually kept gloved in public. Even from that distance the empty sheaths between his pinkie and forefinger were evident.

"You mean, what with his hand all screwed up?"

"Shhh!"

"He's too far to hear," said Sylvia, but she lowered her voice at the next remark. "Is it true what they say?"

When Elena said nothing, she added, "About his molesting a girl. They say her father cut off his fingers ... plus something else. They say that's why he never married."

"They say! They say! Whenever bad things happen to good people, we blame the victim. I'd expect those cruel rumors from common gossips. But coming from a friend ... "

"Take it easy. Those do-good doctors in college have done a number on you. Besides, if you feel so sorry for the old guy, ask him to come out of the cold."

"You mean give him a ride?"

"Why not? He's going our way. Or are you afraid of those other fingers?"

"Of course not." Elena touched her medallion. "Besides, I need to ask him something about some jewelry."

"If it's about that piece of junk hanging on your neck, do me a favor and don't embarrass us both by asking."

"You don't know a thing about jewelry."

"But I know a few things about men. And that so-called boyfriend of yours is as phony as his passport." She pretended to scratch the medallion with her fingernails. "His name's not worth the tin it's engraved on."

"You're saying he doesn't care for me?"

Sylvia, realizing her candor had turned to cruelty, said nothing.

"Honey, he's too handsome for the both of us combined. Anyway, how long have you known this guy?"

"Long enough."

"Long enough for what?" When she got no answer, she added, "Look, I'm not going to preach. But if something already happened, keep it physical. Let him break your hymen but not your heart."

Elena looked at her closely. "Is it the light, or are you turning a little green?"

Sylvia, who up to now had talked liked an older sister, pulled rank with her age. "You mean green as in inexperienced? I'm not the one who's always asking those dumb questions about love."

"I mean green as in envious. Nobody sings you love songs."

"You mean stuff like that so-called song of desperation?" She mimicked a few notes in a vibrato baritone. "I wouldn't put it past him to have stolen it." She saw her words of advice were like the proverbial pearls, so she changed her tactic. "Fine, then. Let's let loverboy put his money where his mouth is." She glanced at don Vicente, who was still at the curb. "The old man can tell us how much that medallion's worth."

Elena now had second thoughts about her piece. "But he's already retired."

"So? He hasn't forgotten how." With that Sylvia honked the horn and motioned him to the car.

Elena tried to dismiss the gesture but her action only drew his attention further. So when he reached her window, Elena invited him along. "You seem to be going our way, don Vicente."

"Hop in," said Sylvia when he peered inside. "We promise not to bite."

He glanced at Elena's medallion and smiled. "Go ahead and bite. I can see you've got your shots." She could not tell whether he had winked or whether he was blinking from the winter sunlight that bounced off her medallion.

Sylvia saw her opportunity. "By the way, don Vicente, is that medal the real thing?"

He smiled. "It is if you're asking if it's gold-plated."

Elena tried hard to hide her disappointment. "So it's not really gold?"

His smile softened into sympathy. "No, not really."

Elena forced a smile of her own. "So jump in, don Vicente, before the year's over."

Soon they were outside the city limits, in one of the county's worst barrios. Mostly migrants lived there, and several front yards had the carcasses of junked cars with expired northern plates.

"What a topsy-turvy world," said Elena. "In the winter, the Anglo *turistas* come down for the weather, and during the summers, the migrants go up for work."

Don Vicente, who often passed through the area on

his bus rides, double-checked the door locks and windows. "On Christmas Day they found a guy by the side of the road."

"Dead drunk?" asked Sylvia.

"No. Dead dead."

Elena tried to hurry through, but the potholes made it difficult since her car muffler was barely held on by two wires. Finally she had to stop at a traffic light, where a small gang was gathered at the opposite corner. One of the adolescents waved to catch their attention and showed them something in his hand.

"What's he got?" whispered Sylvia. "A marijuana joint?"

"It's a firecracker," said don Vicente.

Sylvia rechecked her door lock. "Don't tell me that's how they rob people these days."

"Just about." Don Vicente explained how the boys had in fact set up a lucrative but legal hold-up: "Give them money and they'll hold a lit firecracker. The more the donation, the longer they hold it." He tried to say it matter-of-factly, but Elena thought she noticed a strain in his voice.

She shuddered. "Who in his right mind wants to see them hold a lit firecracker?"

"In that case you give them money not to. Either way they win."

She agreed. "It's no accident they chose this spot. The old Anglos pass through here on their way to their trailer homes."

After the light turned green Sylvia looked back. "All I can say is, if they're counting on snowbirds for handouts, I hope they have extra hands."

"That's not true, Sylvia. Last semester a Winter Texan took the time to speak to our class."

Sylvia, though, had to have the last word. "That's because talk is cheap."

Up ahead, on either side of the road, was one of the
many trailer parks for Anglo retirees. Their recreation
vehicles came and went at a snail's pace, and the elderly
Anglos bicycling along the curb made it difficult to pass.
Each time Elena slowed down for a driver in front, Sylvia
made it a point of reading aloud the out-of-state license
plate. Finally she exclaimed:

"It must take them half a year to get down here. Why
can't they just stay on their farms up north?"

Elena tapped the wheel to show that if anyone in the
car had a right to complain, it was she. "I don't mind.
Slow drivers don't bother me."

"You're right. Mexicans are the other extreme. And if
a snowbird hits you, at least he has insurance. Mexican
drivers don't stop till they're on the other side."

"So Winter Texans are all farmers. That sounds like a
stereotype if I ever heard one."

"So? To them we're all farmworkers."

Elena pointed to several without coats. "At least
they're a hardy breed."

"If they're so tough why do they all leave the first day
it hits ninety?"

"Ay, Sylvia, you and I live in different worlds."

"Of course. You live in the world of ideas, I live in
the world of Wal-Mart. You don't have to put up with
snowbirds and wetbacks six days a week."

"Mexicans who shop at Wal-Mart aren't wetbacks.
They're middle-class *turistas*."

"Well, they have no class when it comes to dealing with
saleswomen. They order you around like you're the dog's
maid." She added: "But our college girl wouldn't know.
The closest you've gotten to a *mexicano* is that boyfriend

of yours with the snake charmer eyes."

Elena knew that Sylvia meant well, but sometimes her teasing tested the limits of friendship. She watched don Vicente in the rear-view mirror, craning his neck while Sylvia continued to call out out-of-state-plates. Elena slowed down to scan a trailer park for a possible survey site. When she returned her sights to the rearview mirror, the color of the old man's face made her do a double-take.

"Don Vicente! Are you all right?! You look like you just saw a ghost."

It took him some seconds to answer. "I'm fine."

Sylvia turned and streaked his window. "Look. Fog. Maybe those old gringas on their bikes back there caught his eye. Then go for it, *señor*. They're like ripe fruit. Once you get past the blemishes, there's a lot of juice left."

Elena had her own theory about his appearance but kept it to herself.

Finally Don Vicente managed a weak smile and asked, "What time is it?"

Elena showed the band of pale flesh on her left wrist. "My watch gave up the ghost a while back." She carefully eyed the old man's feverish reflection. "Anyway, it's time we went home. Soon the roads'll be full of drunk drivers."

Sylvia reminded her, "We need to get ready for that New Year's Eve party."

Elena sighed at the thought of seeing her boyfriend, but this time it rose heavily. "We have a long night ahead."

Yet bright and early on New Year's Day she was awakened by a soft but persistent knocking at her front door. It was don Vicente. Her roommate let him in with dazed reflexes and without fully understanding his explanation. They immediately awoke, though, when don Vicente placed a stylish woman's watch in Elena's hand.

"I'd like to lend you this. It's my thanks for taking me

along."

She returned his smile with a confused grin, hoping to uncover the joke.

"What's this, don Vicente?"

"It's a watch."

"I know that!"

"Yesterday you said yours was broken."

"I mean, what's the story behind it?"

"Last year a mafioso I'd never seen in my life asked me to fix it. He said he'd come back for it, but he never did. I heard he double crossed his partner and ended up underground. That's the story."

"He disappeared?" said her roommate. "Just like that?"

"How else do people disappear?"

Elena took the watch and studied the logo. "Think it's stolen?"

"Why else would he bring it to me instead of a jewelry store?"

She admired it from an arm's length. "It's a pity it's hot." All the while, though, she knew she'd like to have it.

"Well, I can't sell it. And obviously I can't wear it. So if someone doesn't use it it'll just stay hidden between my undershirts."

"What if the guy suddenly pops up?"

"He won't, unless he's in a very shallow grave."

"What if he's still alive?"

"I'll tell him it's in a safe place. Then I'll have to take it back from you. I just figure it's a shame nobody is using it after I fixed it up. I'd like for you to use it for now, at least."

His argument won her over. "How can I ever repay you?"

Don Vicente had a ready answer. "There is one favor I'd like. Another ride. I'd like to look for an old friend."

"A friend?"

"Actually, an acquaintance. I heard he might be living by where you took us. I haven't seen him in years."

"Are you sure he's still alive?"

Her question had an unintended edge to it and she was looking for a graceful way to continue when he answered:

"No, I'm not sure. But if he's still alive after all these years, today's a good day to visit, don't you think?"

She still had a minor hangover from the previous night's party and was in no mood to go. But she was getting used to the watch on her wrist, just as she was envisioning showing it off to her friends. Before any second thoughts could compromise the opportunity, she said, "Sure. Let's do it."

She took an ice cube tray from the freezer, cracked a few pieces and placed them over her eyes.

"Not cold enough for you?"

She removed them and smiled. "Hard night."

He placed his left thumb to his lips and extended his little finger; the missing digits added to the outline's realism. Still, it took her a second or two to trace the silhouette, a while longer make sense of it.

"Oh, not that." She dabbed her eyes where the ice had melted, then felt for puffiness. "Not that much, at least. It's just that I ... stopped seeing someone." She tried to fidget with her medallion and remembered she had returned it the night before. Then, before he could offer his sympathy, she added, "Anyway, they say time heals all wounds."

He simply watched her, neither agreeing nor disagreeing, and she wondered whether wisdom was not so much advice as silence.

With most people she had the distinct impression that
each act was the end result of a succinct, simple thought.
With don Vicente she didn't have that sense. Each gesture seemed part of an intricate sequence, like the meshed
springs and balances that moved a clock's hands. He
seemed to observe people the same way: whenever Elena
talked to him, he seemed to listen less to her words than
for the tiny gears whirring inside. If anyone knew what
made people tick, she thought, it had to be him.

She stepped outside in jeans and a cotton shirt but
quickly went back in for a coat. "Some days that sun's
little more than a light bulb in the sky."

He put on his gloves with an agreeing gesture, tugging
them snugly as they stepped outside. "On days like this I
could swear I feel all my fingers." What he felt was pain,
but nonetheless there was still feeling. "You're the one
with the education, *muchacha*. Why is that?"

"It's called a phantom limb."

Her answer, while not really an explanation, was for
the time being sufficient. "Phantom," he said, spellbound
by the thought that his amputated fingers might still be
floating around somewhere, haunting the world like a flock
of miniature ghosts. "Phantom fingers."

Elena warmed up the car. "So, don Vicente, what's
your friend's address?"

"I can't say exactly."

"Not exactly a close friend, then."

"Not exactly."

She followed the same route as on the previous day
until they reached the rundown barrio, where the gang of
boys stood at the same intersection. The morning chill
was responsible for the presence of only a small hard core
that seemed even more determined. Elena sped up to
catch the green light, but it changed just seconds before

she reached the corner. When her better nature made her brake, her attempt to slip past was not lost on the boys.

"What's the rush, chula?" yelled one.

Another added, "Want to light my firecracker?" He approached the car, a fistful of firecrackers in one hand, a glowing fuse lighter in the other.

Don Vicente buttoned his jacket and rolled down his window. "You're going to lose your hand."

"No I won't." To prove his point, he held the lighter to the fuse with an almost bored pose.

The sight seemed too painful for the old man. "Don't."

"Says who?"

But before don Vicente could answer, the boy tossed away the lit firecracker a split second before it disintegrated with a deafening bang. He dug his fingers in his ears to stop the ringing, then repeated: "Says who?"

Don Vicente rested his gloved left hand on the window's edge.

"What's he got there?" said a boy in back. "A hand puppet?"

Two or three boys came closer, hypnotized by the limp, leather sheath trembling in the wind. One of them insisted, "What's the trick?"

Saying nothing, don Vicente peeled away his glove and spread his fingers to make the mutilation more obvious.

But a cynic in back had a ready answer. "He's probably been that way all his life."

"Right. Like my cousin Tavo."

Don Vicente slowly shook his head and cranked up the car window. "Youth. It only learns from its own mistakes." For a moment he seemed to recall his own younger days. "Sometimes not even then."

"Let them celebrate, don Vicente."

"What? Their right to maim themselves?"

"No.  Another year.  You've collected a few in your time."

He dug his hands deep into his coat pockets.  "You don't collect years, *muchacha*.  You only lose them."

She agreed with the thought, but only abstractly.  Because when she took in the crisp, clean light of that winter morning, it seemed she would remember the sight for the rest of her days.

They drove in silence for a while until Elena brought up the question she had been dying to ask.  "Maybe I'm being nosy, don Vicente ... "  When he said nothing to stop her, though, she continued: "When you warned those boys against playing with fireworks ... Was that from personal experience?"

"What makes you say that?"

"Well, you never said anything about your, ah, handicap before.  And yesterday, when I took you back home sort of sick ... it was soon after we saw those boys.  Then today you asked me to bring you back ... "

"You can certainly add things up.  Did you learn that in college?"

"Sort of."

They rode in silence until he said, "Well, I'm afraid you failed."

"So then you really came to visit a friend?"

He looked straight ahead, so that Elena could not tell if he were squinting or almost smiling.

"Yes."  Then he gave a faint smile.  "But at this rate we'll both be dead by the time I find him."

His reply only whetted her curiosity, and the farther they drove, the more remote she thought her chances were of ever finding out.  Finally she blurted out:

"So when did it happen?"

Not only did the question fail to catch him off guard,

he seemed to have been expecting it. "One summer in South Dakota."

"Which summer was that?"

"My last." He said nothing more for a few seconds, but she knew enough about interviewing to wait him out.

"I was learning to fix farm machinery." He cocked his head back as if he were looking far into the distance. "Learning, hell, I was damned good with my hands. Anyway, to make a long story short, I was trying to get a tractor going when I stuck my hand in the wrong place at the wrong time."

"Whose fault was it?"

"My own, or maybe nobody's. Maybe if I'd been more careful ... or maybe not."

For Elena it was as though a deep mystery had been solved. All those years she had heard incredible accounts of his misfortune. Now the truth was so prosaic that it seemed the strangest of all.

"It must have been terrible ... seeing your fingers lying there ... "

"Oh, I didn't lose them then and there. That happened later, when the grower refused to let me see a doctor."

"Refused?! Why?!"

"He was afraid."

"Of what?"

He looked away, as if the reason no longer mattered.

"Afraid of what, don Vicente?"

"Some said it was the law; others, his insurance company. I was a farm hand. I had no business trying my hand at being a mechanic. A few days later I told him not to worry, that I barely felt a thing any more. I saw him turn a sickly color, like my fingers. So he paid me for the week I'd missed and the next one too. He even advanced me for the remainder of the season."

"Sounds like he was setting you up, señor."

"Back then I thought I was being set for life. I'd never had so much money in my hands."

"So then?"

"So then he gave the crew boss orders to bring me straight to Texas without stopping. 'You're getting the VIP treatment, Chente,' the crew boss told me all the way down. 'All we need's a police escort.' He even had instructions to cover my medical expenses. But by the time we got here it was already pruning season. By then my hand was so swollen, I was relieved to see the dead fingers go."

"Did you ever go back?"

"What for? To get my fingers back? He'd probably tell me they don't grow on trees."

"But you could have sued him."

"The damage was done. I'd never be a mechanic. And in court I'd always be a *mexicano*."

He finished on the same stoical note he had begun. But something told her that if the physical damage had been done, the emotional healing had not.

"Look at the bright side. It got you out of being a migrant.

"That's what some said. Others said I'd been too cocky, helping out the grower, and it cut me down a notch." He added after a while, "So I ended up a watch repairman. It's odd, though. You lose half the fingers of one hand, but the rest are just as nimble."

"So where to now, don Vicente?"

He needed no time to think it over. "Keep going."

Minutes later he pointed to a mobile park up ahead. "Turn here."

"We can't. It's a private road."

He placed his gloved hand on the steering wheel. "I
know. Let's take it."

It occurred to her then that he knew exactly where he
was going. "Oh. A short cut."

"Of sorts."

They entered slowly and in silence. Whenever she
passed by places like this, she felt she was near a cemetery.
When she was younger those trailers had resembled rows
of monumental, aluminum tombstones from a distance.
But today, seeing the fruit-laden citrus trees by each one,
she could not help but wonder whether death felt more at
home in the barrio they had just passed.

She drove past mobile homes and recreation vehicles,
impatient with her snail's pace but careful not to go past
the posted speed limit. "The last thing we need is to run
over an old Anglo," she said.

Don Vicente closely watched both sides of the road,
and when the window's glare hit his eyes, he lowered it
for a better view.

Elena was wondering whether the morning air might
prove too chilly for him when suddenly he asked:

"What's that song?"

She braked and lowered her own window, but the car's
noisy valves masked the music until she turned off the engine. It came from an outdoor loudspeaker by the recreation center, and she waited for the northern breeze to
pick up the scratchy recording.

"Auld Lang Syne."

"What's it mean?"

"It means ... ," she thought back to a distant class
lecture, "old long since." She could tell the literal trans-
lation made little sense. "It's about old times. The good
old days."

"Ah," he said, his nostalgia tinged with bitterness.

"The good old days."

Elena turned the key. The engine started to turn over, then it died. "Oh, shit, Dolores! Not now!"

She pumped the gas pedal a few times but only made it worse. A few elderly Anglos stood on either side of the street and stared, but when no one approached, she felt even more like a trespasser.

She glanced at her passenger. Don Vicente stared straight ahead, as though he could crank up the car with his thoughts.

Her open window was facing north so she raised it, but the anxiety still made her shiver. Turning the key again, she made several attempts at starting the car, until the gas fumes made her stop. "It's flooded." She closed her eyes and threw back her head. "We'll have to wait it out."

It was then that she noticed the open door where the fumes had entered, but no sign of don Vicente.

She stepped out and saw a flock of elderly Anglos around a shuffleboard court, and a smaller group a few yards farther up. Her momentary fear that she might lose him in the crowd was unfounded: his dark face stood out almost immediately, and she began hurrying toward him.

He in turn had already reached the far end of the shuffleboard court and now stood inside its outer stripe. The player, wearing a white *guayabera* and a healthy tan, straightened up from his stoop and smiled. When that did not work he stared hard at the intruder. That tactic also failed to budge him, so he decided to ignore him altogether and pushed the stick in one hard stroke.

The disk was about to skid past when don Vicente stopped it with his shoe, with the natural grace of a cat trapping a mouse in its paw.

Elena arrived seconds after the puck, and the old man with the cue stiffened and yelled: "Does he understand

English?!"

But she seemed as bewildered as everyone else and could only stare back.

"Do you speak Mexican, then? Tell him to get off our court!"

But even had she told him, she doubted he would have heard. He began to walk, oblivious to everything in his path, and for a moment she feared the worst. A few feet in front, immovable and gaunt, stood a grim-faced man holding an upright shuffleboard stick. He had the immutable air of someone who never blinked; one look at him and she thought of the man in "American Gothic".

But at the last instant he stepped aside. Don Vicente continued until another Anglo in short sleeves met him halfway and raised his hand, somewhere between a handshake and a peace greeting.

He told the others he knew Spanish, then said something that made no sense to Elena. Her only clue was his smile.

But after several tense seconds passed, his warm smile gradually froze on his face. He turned unusually pale, even for a Winter Texan, and Elena started to worry, as much for him as for themselves. The stillness all round made it difficult to speak up, but she finally found her voice. "The poor man needs a tan, don Vicente. You're blocking the sun."

The snowbird shivered slightly but kept smiling.

"You're making him nervous," she said, speaking more for herself than for the old Anglo.

Then, without taking his eyes off the smile, don Vicente called out, "Ask him if he remembers."

"Remembers what?" When she asked again, her anxiety was obvious. "Remembers what, don Vicente? He's old enough to remember the Alamo."

"Ask him."

But before she could work up the will to ask, don Vicente ungloved his left hand and thrust it out. The brusque gesture seemed less a greeting than an order to turn back. Elena could have sworn it never touched his opponent, who stumbled backwards in fear.

For a moment he was swallowed by the flesh of his friends. Finally he reappeared at the other end of the crowd, where two men guided him toward a trailer directly across the street. Elena walked a ways behind them, unable to figure out whether they were keeping him on his feet or simply protecting him.

At first she tried to distance herself from don Vicente without drawing attention to the action, but after she saw herself surrounded by strange faces she quickly sought him out. He was almost to the car, and his innocent pace made him seem a bystander rather than an instigator.

She scrambled into the car and managed to fish out her keys from her tight jean pocket. "Let's pray the car starts."

Don Vicente seemed in the best of spirits. "Don't worry. We've got plenty of people to help us push."

She looked in the rear view mirror and saw a small group approaching. When her car started, they quickened their steps. She tried to leave them in a trail of screeching, smoking tires but she caught herself, thanking her good fortune when the car lurched away.

She kept checking the rear mirror until the trailer park disappeared from sight. Don Vicente, though, did not bother looking back even once, and that angered her even more.

"What on earth got into you, don Vicente?"

"I didn't lay a finger on him. You're my witness."

Her stomach cramped at the thought of anything remotely associated with the law. "You didn't have to touch him. You pick on some poor old man who never did anything to you, spook the hell ... "

"But he did."

"He did what?"

"Do something."

"No he didn't. All he did was offer you his hand. I was right there."

"You were there right now. Not back then."

"Back when?"

"Didn't you see the plates?"

"Plates?"

"The plates on the trailer."

"Sure I did. But what ... ?" Suddenly her mouth opened but no words came out. It remained open until she managed to ask, "You mean ... ? Are you sure? Don Vicente, are you sure?"

"Didn't you see? He turned white as a ghost."

"Oh, great! That only describes nine-tenths of all Anglos. Christ, even I turned white as a ghost!"

"It was him," he insisted. When he realized he would never convince her to look beyond what her eyes saw, he tried a twisted logic. "If they're all alike then it doesn't matter. One gringo's as good as another."

"God! If he ever comes to ... And if he doesn't come to ... "

"Don't worry. Either way we'll never see him again."

He removed his other glove and made himself comfortable. Eyes closed, hands clasped on his lap, he seemed at peace with himself.

She watched him intently, on and off, for a long time, hoping he would say something. But his breathing became deeper. Elena thought he was fast asleep when she heard his voice, almost a whisper, saying, "He remembered me."

# The Heart of the Beast

## I

Arturo's first instinct when he woke that Monday was to affirm he had not turned into a dog. Convinced that the fuzz on his cheeks was not abnormal for a boy of ten, he began singing a song to dispel the notion that his voice had been replaced overnight by a bark. Then, angry at himself, he insisted aloud, "People can't turn into animals."

His calf where the dog had bitten him two days ago still felt tender. Hearing his grandfather in the next room where his mother and grandmother slept, Arturo slipped the door's bolt in place. From inside an old shoe box, and with the demeanor of a physician rummaging through his satchel, he produced a roll of thin, glossy tape and began to bandage the tender flesh where the dog had bitten him.

There was a sharp rap on the door. "Wake up, *huevones*!" hollered his grandfather. His insides turned cold, but he managed to bury the tape under a blanket, crouching until the old man walked away. With the same red tape his mother used to seal carrot bags at the packing shed, he wrapped the wound a second time, tight as a tourniquet. Arturo used the tape for playing, although decorating his face and torso like war paint was no longer allowed. The week before, he had stuck racing stripes on his grandfather's wheelbarrow, and don Marcelo had confiscated almost every roll.

Someone pounded on the door, harder than before, this time rattling the knob. "What's going on in there?!" a voice demanded.

"Nothing." His heart almost slipped out between syllables. "I swear."

His cousin's distinctive laugh came through, followed by a sarcastic echo: "Nothing. I swear."

"Get lost, Tomás."

"You thought it was *papá grande*, didn't you? Better wipe the shit from your pants."

"So you can eat it?"

"*Papá grande* heard you. He's right beside me."

After some hesitation, Arturo called his cousin's bluff. "He can eat it too."

Tomás' attempts to impersonate their grandfather no longer sounded convincing. So, now he had started to threaten Arturo by pulling rank, but without success. Tomás was almost a year older than Arturo and had lived with their grandparents for six years, while Arturo and his mother had moved in only four months ago, after the divorce.

Tomás continued pacing outside the door, and Arturo waited him out, rubbing his bleary eyes. He had passed most of last night fretting and tossing on the floor of the room he shared with his uncle Chacho, who usually spent his evenings elsewhere. Arturo took pride in sleeping alone, more so since his cousin never went to bed if their grandfather was not present in the same room. But last night he had missed the security of his uncle's snores. The silence had allowed the whistling of night birds and the terror of his own thoughts to keep him awake, fearful that the dog bite would give him the rabies.

At one point, after being jarred awake by the weight of something crushing him, Arturo's first thought was that his uncle was trampling him in a drunken bout. But finding himself alone, he noticed that the clock indicated it was after three in the morning and he had crawled into Chacho's bed.

## II

It began Saturday, when he was going house to house distributing handbills on Bernal's supermarket specials. On his side of the street, on the corner, stood the sprawling Martínez home. He was almost at the door when a small dog guarding the entrance began barking furiously. From across the street his partner Rafa waved him back. "Forget them. They only shop in gringo supermarkets."

But his cousin, leaf-letting a street perpendicular to his, shouted, "I'll tell Bernal you're skipping houses." When Tomás saw what was holding Arturo back, he gave a belly laugh. "Don't tell me you're afraid of a little thing like that."

"Let's see you try it."

Tomás ignored the challenge. "What a pussy!"

By now what had originated in their classroom had turned into a ritual—Tomás setting up the obstacles, Arturo taking up the dare. For the past several months, both had waged a fierce but undeclared rivalry for the attentions of Lydia López. By now Tomás had extended the battlefield to bait him at every turn of the road, and on each occasion Arturo responded as if Lydia were somehow admiring him offstage. He imagined her now, her large brown eyes secretly looking at him. Meanwhile Tomás had not relented. "Pussy!"

Pressed between the sword and the wall, he armed himself with a rock. With any luck the animal would take the hint and save them both a lot of trouble. But the Martínez mutt growled uncomfortably close, bound as much to its canine instincts as he to his macho rituals.

It took every bit of courage just to fold the handbill and tuck it in the door handle. Arturo was almost across the lawn, pretending that there was nothing to it, when the dog stole up, then grabbed his leg with its mouth. The first sting was not the bite but the humiliation of his cousin's glee. Too late to hit the fleeing dog, Arturo hurled the rock at Tomás which caught him solidly on the left buttock. Tomás hobbled to the curb, sat down and taunted, "Didn't feel a thing!"

Arturo stood across the corner, examining the damage. His first regret was seeing a small tear in his pants.

A gang of boys riding their bikes had witnessed the incident, and the smallest reached him first, imitating an ambulance: "AHHAARRR!"

Tomás, one arm raised in a gesture of goodwill, approached and reminded him, "We're even now."

Arturo rolled up his pant leg. There were two punctures: one fang had hardly broken skin, the other had drawn several drops of blood. One boy suggested to the others, "We'll have to suck out the poison."

"Don't be an idiot," said his older brother. "It was a dog, not a snake." There were several nervous chuckles, then the younger boy said something that made everyone freeze: "What if the dog had rabies?"

Arturo did not need to glance up to confirm the mixture of fascination and sympathy on their faces; the silence was enough. His eyes filled up with tears, as much from rage as from being pitied, and when the tears began to roll down his face, he held on to his calf with both hands and issued a cry of pain as he looked at Tomás. "It's your fault, you stupid jerk!"

"Why me?!" asked his cousin, genuinely scared. "It's Bernal's fault. Sue the pants off him."

His friend Rafa said, "Your mother better take you to the doctor."

His head jerked from side to side in a reflex. "NO!" It was entirely out of the question. His grandfather would never forgive this blunder. "No," he repeated, then enunciated with emphasis, "I don't want anyone to know at home." He stared at his friend, lingering especially long on Tomás, until he got an unspoken oath from each boy.

"Relax," said the boy who had first mentioned rabies. "He probably wasn't even sick."

"Of course he was!" said another. "I saw stuff coming out of his mouth."

Arturo looked him straight in the eyes. "Swear to God?"

The boy looked away. "Father Coronado says it's a sin to swear."

Someone finally concluded: "Well, Arturo, if you're still around in a few days we'll know the dog wasn't rabid."

Just then Bernal's produce manager came to round up the boys in the delivery pickup, and they immediately told him the news. The manager realized the potential for a lawsuit, but he managed an impassive expression. "Why, this is nothing," he remarked on seeing the bite, even seeming a bit peeved at the fuss. "Just rub a little dirt and saliva on it." Still, back at the store Arturo received a little extra money even though he had not finished the route. The manager also volunteered some advice. "If I were you, I wouldn't tell at home. You know parents— they won't let you out of the house for days."

Arturo had nodded in mute agreement.

## III

Now, having survived two full days and going on his third, Arturo had yet to change his mind about the bite. His real dread was his grandfather's reaction to the news. The old man had claimed for some time that his grandson had an uncanny propensity for mishaps, even noting in his almanac the occasion and expense of every sprain, cut and nosebleed since Arturo had come to stay. The tally went back the full four months following his parents' divorce. In actuality not one cent for the medical bills came from his grandfather's pocket, for child support and his mother's job at the packing shed more than covered their share of costs. But that never kept his grandfather from expressing the sentiment that Arturo's so-called accidents were a drain on the household nest egg.

The family doctor, also noting Arturo's accident proneness, had explained how emotional readjustment could cause a sudden rash of injuries. While restitching a gash in a forearm that had reopened after an attempted bike stunt, the doctor had advised that the family at least place Arturo under the school's accident policy. Don Marcelo had sternly opposed it. "Insuring his ass will only encourage more accidents."

So that morning three days after the bite, a preoccupied Arturo tidied his uncle's sheets, then became momentarily baffled by the damp spot in the middle of the bed. He scanned the ceiling for leaks, then he realized with a fierce blush that there was another possible explanation. "Damn!" he told himself. "I'm already pissing everywhere, like a dog."

Only afterwards did it occur to him he might have sweated profusely the night before. But by the time he ran a hand over his back, he was already perspiring. To be on the safe side he decided to change sheets. Yet he almost placed a clean sheet over the same wet circle before he collected his wits and turned the mattress over.

Before he entered the kitchen, he knew his mother was still sleeping, for she had returned from the packing shed after midnight. Tomás, having helped himself to Arturo's cereal box, greeted him a with a smug smile. "Your mother said I could have some anytime I wanted."

Don Marcelo waited until Arturo started eating, then ordered, "Go tell your uncle he'll be late for work."

"He didn't get in last night."

"Why must everyone in this house cover up for him? I peeked through the keyhole this morning. He was tangled in the sheets, having a nightmare."

"That was me," Arturo said meekly.

"That's all we need! Another loudmouth in the house!"

Arturo's grandmother, rinsing vegetables on an outside spigot, peeped through the screen door, "What's wrong, Marcelo? Can't stand the competition?"

"A brawler and a drunk," he mumbled. "Who knows how all this will affect Tomás."

"That's not too difficult to figure out," said doña Elena, "if it's true that history repeats itself." When don Marcelo reacted with a puzzled look, she sprayed him through the screen with a flick of rinsed celery stalks. "Don't tell me your memory's that short."

"But I've changed. I've been setting an example for Tomás, yet Chacho refuses to profit from my mistakes. You really should talk to him, as a mother—I just don't want Tomás picking up bad ideas." He rubbed his grandson's hair with as much affection as his nature allowed. "Of all my grandchildren, I picked the most promising one in the litter. A real go-getter. He'll take care of his *papá grande*."

"Arturito's also becoming a hard worker," doña Elena responded. "He even earned an extra dollar Saturday."

Don Marcelo did not seem impressed. "You have to get them young," he insisted, "the way we got Tomás. That woman would have ruined him if we hadn't taken him in when we did."

He never referred to Tomás' unwed mother as his daughter. When he had offered to raise Tomás, don Marcelo had promised her visitation rights, all the while counting on her lack of concern to wither the ties. What he had not expected was Tomás' own unwavering initiative.

Suddenly reminded of his mother, Tomás said, "I'll go see mamá after school."

Don Marcelo sighed, then commented to his wife, "I wish he wouldn't see so much of her."

"Why not?"

"She doesn't exactly go out of her way to be with him."

"It doesn't bother him. Besides, he needs a mother's affection."

"With all the men she sees, I doubt she has enough left over."

Arturo excused himself. Then don Marcelo noticed his slight limp. "Lose a horseshoe?"

"Huh? Oh, my leg fell asleep."

Tomás imitated his exhaustion. "That's not the only part of you that's asleep."

"Let's have a look," said don Marcelo. "Raise your pant leg." Tomás and Arturo looked at each other.

From a distance don Marcelo examined the constricted, discolored flesh. "No wonder it's numb. You've cut off the circulation." He added, "How this boy loves to mutilate himself. Mark my words, he'll be covered with tattoos by the time he's fifteen."

Arturo yanked off the strips and carefully concealed the bite while don Marcelo warned "I've told you I-don't-know-how-many-times. Don't bind yourself with that damn tape. You're asking for gangrene in some limb. Suppose you end up like 'Peg-leg' Salinas, just dead weight for your family?"

## IV

Arturo timed his arrival at school until just before the tardy bell, but a few stragglers were still on the playground. The news had traveled fast and, seeing Arturo approach, even the loudest boy among them became quiet as though he were witnessing a miracle. Meeting Arturo halfway he confessed, "I almost didn't bother to come today. I was sure we'd be getting a holiday to attend your funeral."

Arturo brushed him aside. "Who says there's anything wrong with me?"

"Nobody has to," said a girl he didn't even know. "You can tell by looking."

The moment he took his seat by the windows, between José Luis Méndez and Oscar Ramírez, his celebrity status became apparent. During third period geography class, at the insistence of Nacho Ayala, he nonchalantly revealed his calf. Students as far as the fourth row craned from their seats to look at the wound.

He did not go home for lunch as was his custom. A half-dozen boys remained by his side. They treated him to a pineapple snowcone from a nearby *tendajo*, then spent the remainder of the lunch hour talking to Santiago Ríos, a patrol boy on duty as well as a veteran of the sixth grade, which he had repeated twice. In addition, his yellow helmet and vinyl shoulder belt gave him an air of worldly authority. Santiago, one of the last students to find out about Arturo's situation, added his own horror story to the conversation: "My father had a cousin in Mexico who was bitten by a rabid animal."

Arturo was almost afraid to ask. "And what happened?"

"In a few days he started frothing at the mouth." Santiago moved his fingers around his mouth. "Later the barking attacks came."

That was the last straw for Arturo. "Barking attacks?"

"Swear to God." He kissed his fingertips. "After the barking attacks, he had to be tied up. They called in the local dogcatcher and had him destroyed."

Someone asked breathlessly, "For real, did he turn into a dog?"

"He was barking. What more do you want?"

Arturo barely gulped. Up to then, his fear of turning into a dog had seemed to be his own private preoccupation. But now, there was hearsay to the contrary. Moreover, the one redeeming consolation for his death—Lydia López weeping by his coffin, confessing her secret love—lost its romantic appeal as he pictured himself dressed in frills and a little party hat, the way performing dogs were dressed on television.

Rafa asked, "Isn't there anything they can do?"

Arturo was surprised that his friend still harbored a shred of hope, and even more amazed when the patrol boy answered, "Sure!" Santiago's pubescent voice was full of excitement. "That's what angers my papá now. He says in those days people were too pigheaded. They could have taken his cousin for treatment—"

"What kind of treatment?"

"Shots—they stick over a dozen shots in your stomach."

The thought was enough to make everyone wince. San-

tiago drove home his point by poking the staff of his traffic
flag at Arturo's belly a few times. Someone said what they
were all thinking, "You'd have to be crazy to say yes to
that."

"They're like a bunch of vaccines," added Santiago,
"and they hurt *chingos*."

"Where do you get those vaccines?" asked Arturo.

"From cattle." Santiago tried scratching his head to
stimulate additional information, then realized he was still
wearing his helmet. "It's something like cow blood."

Arturo clarified his question: How could he get his
hands on the antidote? "From a doctor. Where else?"

He was back to where he had started. The mere men-
tion of a doctor meant that at some point his grandfather
would find out. Almost as an afterthought he considered
another possibility: "And what happens after you're given
that cow crap?"

Someone else must have read his fears: "You turn into
a *vaca* instead of a dog."

No one could resist laughing, and one boy mooed. But
Santiago was quick to point out, "*Vaca pero vivo.*" Even
if he turned into a cow, he'd still be alive.

Returning to class, Arturo noticed a cluster of girls
looking his way. Lydia was among them. Rafa explained:
"They heard you're dying from rabies, but that you refuse
to see a doctor."

Detecting what seemed like admiration in Lydia's
glances, he responded with the studied grimace of someone holding back racking pain. "And what do they say to
that?"

"They say you're crazy."

Just before class he told Tomás, "If you happened to
tell at home, I wouldn't get mad."

"*Papá grande* would."

His voice lowered to an urgent whisper to sound more convincing. "I can't tell him, especially now. He'll kill me twice for having waited so long."

Tomás twisted in his chair to avoid Arturo's gaze. "If there's anything *papá grande* hates worse than a crybaby, it's a tattletale."

His pencils had been taken by souvenir hounds and a crude tombstone had been scratched on his desk top, with the inscription: Arturo de la O—R. I. P. For the rest of the afternoon Santiago's words stayed in his mind. They made sense. Baby monsters were born all the time in Mexico; he'd seen pictures in his grandfather's tabloids. He spent phonics class brooding on the prospect of spending the remainder of his natural life tethered in backyards, chewing on a cud of *quelite* and thinking bovine thoughts. He looked at the bright side: Cattle didn't go to school, and he could supply dairy products to the family table. But eventually, after the novelty of reincarnation wore off, his heart of hearts foresaw a life of beastly boredom.

During history period, Mrs. Bridgeman gave him permission to see the school nurse for a headache. The teacher, who had already been resurrected from retirement once, was totally in the dark as to the gossip and could not fathom the class' collective bated breath when he hurried to the infirmary. As Arturo left the room, Tomás gave a nasal rendition of bugle taps, a mourning usually reserved for students sent to the principals's office.

Arturo was sent home with a temperature. In the absence of children, the streets seemed completely alien, as if grownups put away every bicycle, swing and monkeybar then switched everything back to normal just before school let out. He attributed the headache to his having only a snowcone for lunch, yet he could not get rid of the idea that this was the first symptom of rabies. He braced himself for the inevitable moment: When the end came, how would it come? Maybe he'd succumb in stages, following the sequence set down in every werewolf movie; he realized he needed to consult his grandfather's almanac for the night of the next full moon.

At home doña Elena maternally felt his forehead with the back of her hand, put him to bed and prepared *man-zanilla* tea. "This poor little soul is burning with fever."

"He's faking," insisted don Marcelo.

"How can anyone fake a fever?"

"This one can. He makes-believe so hard he even convinces himself."

At dinner time he awoke to his uncle's good-natured commotion. He peered in the mirror and was momentarily horrified that the transfiguration had begun. One side of his face was striped from his having slept on top of the chenille bedspread.

Entering the kitchen dazed and disoriented, thinking it was already the following morning, he asked his mother for an excuse from school for the rest of the day. Hearing this, Tomás sputtered what he had been chewing and choked on his laughter.

Arturo's mother cradled his face, stroking the cheek still marked from the bedspread. Her water-wrinkled hands gave out a clean, damp-earth smell from her having handled rinsed carrots all day. "Not feeling well, *hijito*?" Her hairnet told him she had to return to the shed, and he quickly sat next to his uncle.

"Arturito needs a doctor," said doña Elena. "He's still weak from that chill he caught in the rain."

"That's what I hate about the carrot season," said his mother, "working overtime. Well ... Arturo comes first."

"That's the sixth time you've missed," protested don Marcelo, "and for the same reason. You'll get fired."

"What good is money if my son is ill?"

"The only one who comes out ahead is that damn doctor," said don Marcelo. "How many Cadillacs have we
helped him buy already? This doctor must be giving Arturo shots to keep him acting crazy."

"Why so alarmed all of a sudden, Marcelo? It was
you who started brainwashing them with that *muy macho*
stuff. 'Never walk away from a fight, boys, or you'll wake
up without any *huevos.*'"

"Papa hasn't changed a bit," said Chacho. "He used
to tell me the exact same thing." He winked at Arturo.
"Luckily I never paid attention."

"You're both distorting things," said don Marcelo.
"The real trick is not to go crying back to *mami* every
time your thing gets caught in a zipper. That's the one
thing they have to learn, even if it kills them."

"You've almost succeeded in having that happen, too,
Marcelo. The doctor almost has to pull words out of his
mouth. Carmela always goes along because she's the only
one who can coax out his feelings."

Tomás, seeing the chance to jockey for his aunt's attention, said "Mama says it must be awful having a son
who's always going to the doctor."

"What does she know?" muttered Arturo. "She's always drunk."

Arturo's mother glanced at don Marcelo out of the cor-
ners of her eyes. The remark had left him seething. "Arturo, don't ever say that again." Her voice was soft but
stern. "Be grateful for a mother who looks after you. Not
like poor Tomasito." Tomás concealed his smirk inside
his glass of Kool-Aid. But his victory was short-lived, for
the next moment Carmela was feeling Arturo's forehead.
"I'll make a doctor's appointment for tomorrow," she concluded.

Don Marcelo shook his head from side to side and clucked his tongue in disappointment while his wife observed, "Arturito hasn't been himself the past few days."

Secure that his cousin would guard the truth, Tomás said, "I heard that a dog spooked you."

That explained everything for doña Elena. "Of course! *Susto*—he's suffering from fright!"

"Fright?" questioned don Marcelo. "The truth is that this boy is really an ox with tennis shoes—*una res con tenis*. Too bad he's not in India. He'd be sacred there."

Tomás asked, "What does that mean, *papá grande*?"

Don Marcelo positioned himself beside Arturo, whose chest swelled with rage. He tried to stand, but his grandfather yoked his neck under a firm grip. "Step closer and observe!" Don Marcelo gave his voice the edge of a sideshow barker. "The only difference between this child and your ordinary ox is that this one runs around in tennis shoes. As far as gray matter goes, they're tied. Both plunge headfirst into danger with utter dumbness."

Arturo was at the point of slapping away his grandfather's hand when doña Elena exploded. "The only dumb animal in this room is you, Marcelo! Squandering money earned by the sweat of our children to entertain friends in *cantinas*. Look what it left us—a crumbling shack. You should've been a tightwad back then. Now all you're good for is picking on innocent children." She turned to Arturo's mother. "Fela the *curandera* can cure his *susto*. That woman performs miracles."

Don Marcelo, who had not been consulted, gave his consent as a face-saving gesture. "At least she's cheap."

That evening Arturo answered Fela's inquiries while she felt the tonicity in his wrists and elbows. She finished her ritual of prayer and brushes with *estrafiate* branches but even then she detected the lacklust er look in his eyes.

"It took more than a dog's barking to jolt him this badly."

"I already gave him three cups of *manzanilla* tea," said doña Elena.

"You'll have to brew a whole kettle before this is over." He half-hoped she might guess his secret. Perhaps she even had a special prayer for rabies. "This little creature of God is still hiding something ... " Her pronouncement carried a serenity that put him at ease. That instant a *lechuza* shrieked as it flew over the house, and Fela's concentration snapped. When she recovered, she looked like someone trying not to demonstrate fear. "Things are getting bad," she half-whispered. "Now she doesn't even wait till midnight."

His mother whispered back, "Who?"

Fela raised her voice slightly as if to stay one step behind the hearing range of the *lechuza.* "That attractive *morena* who just moved down the block. They say she's a *bruja.*"

"What's she have against you?"

"Several women have been terrorized by whistling noises at night. Each one thinks the witch is after her, and each one wants me to step in. So far I haven't, but now it seems the young lady wants to get the jump on me." She took out a yellow silken cord from a chiffonier. "You're welcome to stay if you like, but it might get frightening."

Doña Elena led the way to the front door, lingering long enough to add, "I don't know anything about the whistling, but she does have every male over six in the vicinity like a dog in heat. Soon this barrio will be nothing but broken homes, like ours."

She glanced at Arturo's mother. "I've already lost one son-in-law that way."

Fela's murmur made him more aware of the dark, of the way cricket chirps thickened the night's hush. "In that case be careful with Marcelo. Sorcery respects no one," she said.

Arturo spent the remainder of the night locked in his uncle's room, gazing through a window that faced the street. From his unlit vantage point he could see a trickle of curious children edging along the picket fence at a snail's pace, peering without success into his quarters, and he also saw three of four bicycle riders cruising back and forth, whistling softly.

Early the next morning, Arturo surveyed the bleak playground as he pretended that he had survived into the summer. Rafa arrived with the others and reported the news at once. "Yesterday we tossed the Martínez mutt a poisoned weiner. We heard it moan all night, spooky moans, like a human. Today his hind legs were already stiff."

Arturo managed a detached gratitude, despite someone's observation that they had killed any chances for finding out if the dog were actually rabid. That comment was met with cynical asides, for now it was assumed the mutt had been rabid. Rafa asked, "Did I mess up, Turi?"

He shook his head no, adding half-heartedly, "Thanks for helping me get even."

Someone's arm brushed his back, and a girl moved forward nervously among her friends, partly pushed in his direction, partly on a dare. His reputation must have grown, for today the perimeter of gawkers had expanded. From the start, after the experience with doña Fela became known, Tomás had begun whining and panting like a puppy until the joke wore on everyone's nerves. Then when Lydia was within earshot, Tomás inquired, "And what excuse did the *curandera* give you? That you had *susto*?" He drew closer for the next remark. "As soon as you're gone," he hissed in Arturo's ear, "I'm taking your place with your mother."

The next instant Tomás was on the ground, and Arturo mounted him. As he flipped his cousin on his stomach a girl cautioned, "Don't let him bite you, Tomás. He'll give you rabies."

"Shut up! Don't give him ideas!"

Smiling, Arturo traced a moist finger across his captive's neck and licked the residue. "Needs salt," he announced. He took a pinch of dirt from an ant hill and sprinkled it on Tomás' nape, then grazed him with his incisors. Tomás bleated in helpless terror. Arturo was swooping in for another nip when his cousin's head jerked backwards. Arturo clenched his teeth the moment Tomás caught him squarely on the nose.

He landed hard on his tailbone. For several seconds he sat dazed, sifting the ant mound with one hand, oblivious to his surroundings. Finally he wobbled to his feet, blood oozing from one nostril and a smear of it on his teeth. Tomás, his right shoulder stained, raised a stiff arm like a club.

The small mob stepped back. Their voices came and went like chants, as if someone were cupping his palms against his ears trying to catch the noise. Tomás, choking, bolted for the main doors only to find them locked.

Most of the spectators stampeded towards the wall and formed knotted circles there for protection. The braver ones simply skipped back a few steps, gingerly testing whether Tomás might charge, then stood their ground. Rafa and two friends were patrolling the no-man's land separating Arturo from the others. Their loyalty shifted with their distance, for they did not know how far to trust him. Barely able to recognize them, Arturo shivered and snorted to clear the grogginess. Someone yelled, "He's going to attack!", and the hysteria that followed cost him his last friends.

It took their grouping against the school wall—some armed with stones—to make Arturo see he was no longer one of them. From now on there were no more enemies, no more friends, no more relatives, no more secret sweethearts. From now on there were only victims to attack.

They began yelling as if to frighten away a wild animal. Tomás was making a sheepish attempt to mingle within the fold when someone gave away his cover by yelling, "The cousin has it, too!" Twice Tomás was physically shunned from their ranks until he settled with prowling just beyond the accurate range of the stone throwers.

At first Arturo wanted to make him see: that it was he alone against everyone else, just as it had always been; that, in the end, being himself came down to the terrible liberty of every man for himself. Then it no longer mattered, for he would discover that on his own in due time.

Arturo faced them with a sobbing laugh. He had never before been so much himself.

# Boys' Night Out

The night promised to stay warm and starry, so the floor show had been moved to the patio of the cabaret. Earlier that evening Ramiro Salazar had crossed into Mexico on the pretext of finding a souvenir for a cousin returning to Illinois the following morning. But, on finding each store already closed, he had strayed from the tourist section of town until he found himself in the hub of the red light district. He had kept telling himself there was no harm in looking. Feeling that life had been passing him by, he loitered outside the cabaret entrance, trying to mask his excitement with the same impassive air of the clientele who walked in and out with jaded faces. The man soliciting him to step inside began to insist. "Take a peek, our girls don't bite."

A woman by the door laughed, so he went inside to save face.

Although he had grown up on the border, he had missed this experience, almost a rite of passage for male adolescents. And all the stories he had heard about *"mala muerte"* nightclubs had not prepared him for the way these men pursued happiness with a grim vengeance.

A man abruptly left a choice seat, and Ramiro asked those at the table if he could join them. One of the Mexicans jerked his head up and stared. "Only if you're Mexican."

He smiled nervously. "I am, but from the other side."

The man said nothing, and Ramiro wondered whether he was daring him or was simply hard of hearing. Then the man's friend banged on the metal seat. "Close enough!"

He sat with the same caution with which he was surveying his surroundings. Only one man had a table all to himself. Thickly mustached, sporting an ornate *guayabera* that bordered on vanity, and with the arrogance of the upper-class, he was bent on proving his manhood to the masses. Ramiro could well imagine that somewhere in the man's past he must have pistol-whipped a servant or forced himself on a maid.

Ramiro sipped a lukewarm beer. Soon a diminutive prostitute cuddled up on his lap. "Who's the stranger with suspicious eyes?"

He told her he was from across the border, worked as a county bureaucrat and had a son with the same eyes. She yawned audibly and left. After that he was no longer approached.

Suddenly a flash popped a few feet away and left him blinded for a few seconds. Then he made out an itinerant photographer a few tables away taking pictures of two adolescents. The more drunk of the two had his arm around his friend. Ramiro inspected the ambulatory photographer until he was satisfied that the man did not have the face of a blackmailer.

The militant Mexican sharing Ramiro's table began such a tirade against anything American that it became impossible for Ramiro to ignore him. "If I were God ...
"

"You're the next best thing, Angel," said his companion. "But you're drunk."

"No, *compadre.*" The Mexican removed his Western hat and raked back his thinning hair, lank as the leather fringes on his deerskin jacket. "If I were God I'd line up the *americanos* against the patio wall and shoot them in the gut, like thieving coyotes. They only come here to screw our women."

His friend, still on this side of sobriety, nudged Ramiro on the sly. "You don't really mean that, Angel."

"I do, *compadre*! These women may be whores, but they still deserve respect."

"Maybe that's what they need, but what they want are dollars. And *americanos* are their best clients." He told Ramiro in a low voice, "It's the do-gooders in this world who cause the most trouble. Like my friend here, the Avenging Angel."

He was interrupted by a fanfare from the band's trumpets. "And now!" said the master of ceremonies. "The debut of the year. The Kiki Club is proud to present ... Sor Juanita!"

The band slipped into a lively *cumbia,* and the audience sat rapt as a slender girl in a nun's habit came on stage. Blessed with an angelic face, she seemed perfect for the role, dancing demurely enough to make the fantasy plausible. Above the crowd's cheers Ramiro even heard someone say, "A pity she's a *puta.*" Even her make-up had the perverse appeal of an angel with a dirty face. But it wasn't until she came quite close that he noticed her eyes, glassy like a doll's.

His suspicion was clinched after someone asked, "And what are you selling under that habit, Sor Juanita?"

For the first time he heard her voice, raw and without subtleties. "Same thing your sister gives for free."

The crowd gasped as if a real nun had cursed, and for a moment the performance teetered between satire and sacrilege.

At the end of the number she shed her habit, leaving a chamois loincloth over her panties. She had only the slightest swell of breasts, but Ramiro heard someone praise her nipples. "Dark as mulberries," said the Mexican named Angel. "And just as juicy, I'll bet."

For her second number she kept the loincloth and slung a quiver over her shoulder, filled with peacock feathers, which she darted at the audience. By then Ramiro had begun to lose interest, but the man named Angel sat ecstatic, the fringes on his cowboy jacket whipping about when he clapped. "My Aztec goddess!" he shouted. His reward was a feather which he went out of his way to snatch, almost knocking over their beers.

She finished the number with her loincloth intact. By the third tune the hardcore crowd, used to complete strips, made its disenchantment known, until the heckles smothered the music. Even the Anglos, who up to now had limited their outbursts to high-pitched hee-haws, joined in the clamor for more flesh.

The commotion finally brought out a heavy-set man from the cabaret proper. "What's all the racket?"

"Your new girl," said the master of ceremonies. "She's making them suffer."

He glanced up from the platform's edge. "You know what they came for."

"That's not what we agreed on," she said, shaking her head.

He struck Ramiro as a man who seldom bothered with life's fine print. "Where do you think you are?" the man said as he left. "The Miss Mexico pageant?"

Just then, prompted by the band, the new girl lurched

into a half-hearted samba. Then the overhead lights were dimmed and she was illuminated with a floor lamp that rotated colors. She shielded her eyes and froze on the spot, the band stumbling a few notes behind her. "What am I, a damn Christmas tree?!"

"You're a damn stripper! Quit stalling!"

Then came a distinct but untraceable voice: "Sor Juana's a sir, isn't he?"

The men immediately murmured among themselves, then questioned the other women. No one seemed to know her. Then the same anonymous voice added, "He stepped out of the closet tonight."

Ramiro tried to stare at Sor Juana's crotch but could not bring himself to steal more than a fleeting glance. The Mexican sweltering in the deerskin jacket stood to placate the audience but was harassed back into his chair. "Hey, mister," someone added, "tell your boyfriend Juan ... " The howls from the audience drowned out what followed.

The man stood, waited until everyone had his fill, then turned to Sor Juana. "Show them you're a woman."

"Who the hell are you? My pimp in shining armor?"

"Show them."

In the hush of the patio, Sor Juana's reply rang even more defiant. "Make me."

The man slipped a hand inside his jacket, and Ramiro heard a crisp snap.

"He's armed!" said someone, and by the time the warning reached the rear, the man had shifted his axis to cover both exits.

Ramiro had no way of knowing how long he and the others simply sat there. He could feel the horde's forced exhaling pressing on his own diaphragm, as he consciously breathed in and breathed out.

Then everyone began to breathe the thin air, filling

their lungs the way one prepares for a plunge of unknown depth. No one uttered a word, but that did not make the panic any less real. If anything, the eerie silence told them that now was not the time to lose one's breath on words.

Into that roomful of suspended animation the cabaret boss returned, as though a vacuum had sucked him in. "Now what? Everyone's on strike?" His voice revived a girl who used his huge frame to slip outside.

The master of ceremonies, paralyzed in his corner, microphone glued to his dry lips, tried to caution his boss. Through a supreme effort he managed an amplified warning that boomed through the void like God Himself: "CAREFUL!"

Helpless among the terrified audience, Ramiro remembered the time a grade school teacher had forced his class to sit through recess, and he wondered whether his past was coming back to him for a reason. Meanwhile the world out there seemed an immense festivity that made the stillness inside all the more maddening. From other *cantinas* and cabarets, polkas and huapangos competed in reckless abandon, and drunken shrieks met their muffled end against the patio wall.

Suddenly someone banged on the patio door. "Open up in there!" For a moment Ramiro thought help had arrived, until the man added, "Why's it so dead?! Is everyone saying a bedtime prayer?!"

A woman betrayed her presence with a cough, and he yelled, "Conchita! I can hear you breathe! I know you're in there with another man! Who's the s.o.b.?!"

"Terrorist!" she hastily called out.

"Tourist?!" the man replied. "I'm no goddamn tourist! I'm Ponciano Valverde, goddamnit! And there's enough pesos in my back pocket to buy all your mothers! Forward and backward!" He threw a bottle over the wall, and it shattered on the floor. "You can all go to hell, for all I care!"

A corrido sounded in the distance, pitting honor against death. It ended in a soulful yell, but the night's immensity shrank it to a tiny yelp.

Hearing sobs, Ramiro had to glance around to make sure they were not his own. That was when he caught the upper-class don slowly raising his *guayabera*. He seemed to be holding his breath—making Ramiro's own chest tighten in suspense—while the rich man's hand crept along his side with the painstaking patience of a lecher feeling up a napping servant girl. Then he exposed the cold gleam of a mother-of-pearl pistol handle. The instant the man gripped the weapon, Ramiro had the absolute certainty he was about to die in the cross fire of two fools.

Discouraging him with furtive head shakes proved useless; he couldn't distract the man's attention from the first gunman. And if he signalled the man next to him, he could trigger a bloodbath, for there was no telling how many more weapons would be drawn.

Suddenly the don covered his gun. But before Ramiro could thank his stars, two policemen stormed on stage. One, disheveled and annoyed as though roused from bed, aimed his ancient Mauser wildly.

Sick with terror, Ramiro turned to a man at the next table. "I shouldn't have come here."

"All this is part of the show," his neighbor insisted, and Ramiro didn't know whether to pity or to envy his intoxicated innocence.

The cabaret boss took a pragmatic tack. "Now, Sor Juana, or whatever your name is. Enough is enough. Stop before you get into real trouble."

Sor Juana's inert expression turned ironical. "Isn't this real enough for you?"

"For God's sake, think of these innocent people. Think of their families." His hand swept the crowd like a mass blessing. As it passed, Ramiro half-raised his own hand.

Sor Juana appraised the standoff for a while, looking at her captive audience a while longer. Then, without waiting for the music, she broke into dance. The drummer and rhythm guitarist followed her paces like frantic amateurs hanging on for dear life, and the sax player was so short of breath he only played in patches. Twice they paused entirely, cuing her to finish. Finally she faced her admirer, rolled down her panties and raised the loincloth.

The Mexican man cracked an embarrassed smile as though the entire episode had been a minor inconvenience, then withdrew his hand to clap politely. Ramiro never found out whether the man was really armed. The cops closed in while the infuriated don brandished his own weapon, offering to assist in any way.

Ramiro tried joining the exodus but had trouble standing. When his legs finally responded, he camouflaged his fear with an exaggerated amble.

Outside he shivered slightly in the balmy evening. His legs, still unsteady, gave the impression he had left his old bones behind.

From his left came a soft, philosophical chuckle. "Well, sir, we're still here, for better or for worse." It was Angel's companion. He handed Ramiro a half-filled bottle. "Borrowed this on my way out." His chuckle turned mischievous. "Let's drink to life."

The brandy burned Ramiro's throat, but it also invigorated him. "Where's your friend?"

"Learning his lesson, I guess." The stranger took back the bottle and offered a toast. "But tonight I made a new one, and the night's still young."

Once again he gave the bottle to Ramiro, who shook

his head but took it anyway. "It's late. I need to head on home."

"What for? The bridge stays open all night."

"Mustn't push our luck. We got out of this one ... "

"And we'll get out of the next one, and the one after that! Don't you see? It's not our turn. Not yet. So live it up!" He clinked the bottle resting on Ramiro's chest with his ring. "Are you going to nurse that all night, *amigo*?"

Against his better judgment Ramiro took a deeper swig and looked up at the stars. It seemed an eternity since he had last seen such a sight, and their distant fire warmed his insides. "Maybe I will join you for a while, until I'm my old self again."

"Well, don't take forever to decide. Life is short."

After a drink or two with his newfound friend, Ramiro was unaware that the lesson that was to last an eternity and alter his life forever had already lost its urgency.

A few hours later, swimming in the here and now of the intoxicated moment, he was having the time of his life.

# Independence Day

The downtown sidewalks were a carpet of blue jeans, khakis and cotton shirts. For the past hour Arturo had been standing underneath a store awning, among the multitude braving the noonday heat for the Fourth of July parade. He was not enjoying the parade as much as he could have, for he was keeping a close watch on the legs of his baggy khakis. In deciding to wear them because they could hold his "monster" firecrackers, he had forgotten a cardinal rule: never wear cuffed pants at a parade. A certain pack of pranksters, it was rumored, went through the crowd with their own little contest—seeing who could drop a lit firecracker into a bystander's pant cuff.

There was the usual collection of spectators: guys trying to pick up on girls; some girls ignoring—others enjoying—the flirting; there were even entire families who had staked out their places the way they did at park gatherings, complete with the obligatory fat aunt. Here and there a few patriots went to the trouble of waving miniature flags some organization had distributed. Most of the flags, though, lay littered on the curb, and no one except a few children collecting them bothered to pick them up.

He slipped into his favorite pastime, filling his lovesick hours projecting his admiration of Lydia López onto any girl with a vague resemblance to her. Every summer that her parents migrated to California, he stayed behind with the fear they might settle there for good. Conjuring her image in her absence was part of his ritual to ensure her return. But today, despite the large pool of near-lookalikes, he was not enjoying himself, and comparing the excitement of other eleven-year-olds with that of their half-bored parents, he wondered whether his own life had already reached a stalemate.

Still, the bathing beauties who flashed their rehearsed smiles his way received a silly grin of gratitude. Several times he told himself he was tired of the game. In the first place, he hadn't asked for a smile; moreover, with his face embedded in the crowd, they couldn't even see whether he smiled back or not; finally, their smiles were nothing special, but rather thrown at random to the crowd. Yet he felt sorry for those who received more indifference than applause, so at the last moment he would crack a smile.

Down the street, on the opposite curb, his friend Rafa and two other boys were not only smiling but welcoming each girl with a tremendous racket. That alone would have kept him away; but the presence of the two boys he did not know added to his distancing, especially since the older of the two had the look of a loudmouth.

He was debating whether to return to the barrio and try out his huge firecrackers when he cast a haphazard glance over his shoulder—and there was Lydia López! Stunned, he tried holding on to the mirage, convinced he had pushed his imagination too far this time. It took him a moment longer to realize it was Lydia, in the flesh. He had not seen her in this lemon-colored dress before, and this time her dark brown hair fell short of her shoulders, but it was her. In contrast to the crowd, glued to the antics of a man in a super hero suit riding a float, her attention was distracted to one side. That modest difference somehow set her apart from the suffocating throng. Her profile was in the clear for only a few heartbeats. Then she seemed to recognize a face and was lost in the mob.

Arturo vowed not to move until he could spot the lemon-colored dress again. But after two floats passed by and she had not yet bobbed into view, he panicked and dove into the crowd.

The mob, only a moment ago as inert as he, all at once turned into a machine set in gear, intent on moving against him. He weaved past opportunities of breasts and bottoms, oblivious even to firecracker terrorists, throwing every sense into the search, sniffing through a swamp of hair spray and deodorant, struggling to screen out yellow hues from the crazy quilt of the crowd. When he suddenly found himself almost an arm's length behind her, he gasped and jumped back a few paces. Then he planted himself squarely behind her, where she would least likely catch him worshipping her.

He drank in her image as though he had been dying of thirst the past few weeks: her swift, direct gestures, her sunburned shoulders, her firm buttocks that seemed to have turned rounder in that one month. After awhile, fearing she might sense his stare, he turned his attention to her guardians, two ladies and a man. The women were both heavy-set but well-dressed, especially when compared to the informality of the crowd. The man, though, was rather tall and very casually dressed. He gave the impression that his lankiness had somehow made him give up on elegance. Of the group, he alone seemed ideal for parade watching, and not only because of his height. He stared like a perched hawk, following the festivities with unblinking eyes until they were beyond anyone else's interest.

"Turi! Turi!"

Arturo looked around: someone was shouting his nickname, but the sheer size of the crowd made it almost impossible to pin the voice to a face. His frustration increased on his realizing that shouting practically obliterated what made a voice unique, so that he did not have a clue as to who could be calling him. Finally he honed in and realized he had ended up almost directly across the street from Rafa.

He pretended to keep looking as if he had not recognized him, but his friend persisted.

Arturo finally tried to dismiss him with a half-hearted wave. But now Rafa, knowing he had caught his attention, turned more insistent, even adding some wild gestures. "Turi! Get your skinny ass over here!"

Finally even Lydia glanced back sternly, as if people with skinny asses annoyed her. One of the women with her also turned, with a look suggesting that whatever bothered the girl bothered her as well. He half-hid behind an adult, and neither one noticed him, but for a moment the faces in the crowd, an instant ago fragmented into a thousand individual concerns, seemed to focus on him.

Seeing no end in sight, and realizing that the loudmouth was no longer around Rafa, he started toward him.

Crossing the street during parade hours was prohibited, so his walk took on a certain defiance. For a moment he relished the role of a rebel, especially in full view of Lydia. Then it occurred to him he might be making a bad impression on her guardians, so midway there he turned his swagger into a stiff stride. Still, he worried that Rafa's publicity had made his skinny ass quite obvious.

Reaching the other side, he was teased by Rafa. "I

didn't know you were marching in the parade."

Rafa introduced him to another boy, his cousin, from another school. Arturo gave him a few firecrackers, the tiny ones he had planned to toss in the parade. Rafa's cousin offered him a candy bar turned soft by the heat, and he had to scrape the chocolate from the wrapper with his incisors.

The boy who had been with Rafa, the same one Arturo had avoided, suddenly rushed to their side, pushing other children aside and using others to block his exit. Seeing him closer, Arturo confirmed his judgment: the boy had that light complexion he sometimes saw in Chicano boys who turned out haughty or just troublesome. Now, though, his face was red, as much from the heat as from running.

Rafa's cousin looked at him with an almost parental air, even though the boy was older. "What did you do this time?"

"Nothing. I've just been exploring."

"He hasn't been around," Rafa's cousin told Arturo. "He just got back."

The boy pretended to hush Rafa's cousin yet waited for him to tell the rest of the story. When he didn't, the boy glanced at him until he added: "He's been in the shade, you know."

The boy checked Arturo's face to make sure he knew that the shade was slang for reform school. Satisfied that Arturo was in the know, he gave him a proud smile. Then he turned serious by degrees, until he said: "I'm never going back."

There was something amiss about the way he insisted, but Arturo could not figure it out until Rafa's cousin said, "Then you better get your shit together. I've told you time . . ."

"I'm never going back," he repeated, and stared so hard at his friend that it seemed Rafa's cousin had actually threatened to take him back.

It was then Arturo realized that when the boy insisted he was never going back, he never intended to get on the straight and narrow, much less stay there. He simply was not going back.

He must have started becoming suspicious of Arturo too, because he turned to scrutinize him with a quiet terror that bordered on danger. At that moment Arturo almost wished the boy would go back to his self-confident, swaggering self.

Rafa's cousin sensed the boy's fright and tried to distract him. "Remember I told you about Arturo?" The mixture of confusion and curiosity on the boy's face encouraged the cousin to add: "Sure, I told you about him, from Rafa's school. The one who took on the whole school when they thought he had rabies."

The boy had been impressed enough by the feat to remember Arturo immediately. For a moment Arturo felt that the boy had given him a special look for a fellow outlaw, a look that both frightened and emboldened Arturo.

The boy was still studying him when he asked abruptly, "You took on the whole school?"

Arturo, still not knowing how to take the dubious honor, opted for humor. "Well ... all except the principal."

It took the boy a second or two to decide he wasn't serious. Then he let out a strange laugh, eerie in its silence punctuated by an occasional high pitch. "Your friend's a funny guy, Rafa!"

The boy stopped to admire another batch of bathing beauties, each blinking into the strong sun and shading her eyes with one hand while throwing blind kisses into the crowd with the other. But after they passed, he began scratching his arms in agitation.

"I'm getting tired of looking," he said. "Let's go feel up some real flesh." He pointed to a spot in the crowd he had already scouted.

Rafa, afraid to lecture him but just as determined not to give in, looked to Arturo for help.

"I'm fine right here," was all Arturo said.

Rafa began staring straight ahead, as if he too were enjoying the view. Finally, desperate to say something, he asked, "Say, Turi, isn't that Lydia from our class?"

Arturo nodded. Even in the scorching sun his face felt damp, as if a nosebleed had betrayed his emotions.

"Linda?" asked the boy. "Her name's Linda? Well, she's a real *linda*, all right."

Arturo wanted to pronounce her name as sweetly as it sounded in his thoughts, but that would be tantamount to confessing his love. "Lydia," he said flatly.

"Introduce me to her."

"She thinks she's hot shit," said Rafa.

Instead of being discouraged, the boy agreed. "She is hot shit. You probably need permission from both women just so you can put your hand on her tits."

"She hardly says 'hi'."

"I don't care if she's mute." He scrutinized her closer for a long while; then, above the approaching din and clatter of some National Guard tanks, he dropped the bombshell: "Oh, I know her! She made it with a gang from our barrio."

Arturo scoffed at the very idea with an incredulous laugh before the tanks could drown him out. But it was obvious no one else held her image sacred. Finally, in an effort to save face, he said, "It must have been her older sister. I caught her after school with a married man."

Actually he had spied them from a distance, behind
a packing shed, while sorting through a crate of rejected
melons. It had been her lover's silken seduction—the
suave way his hand had undone her blouse—that gave
the impression he was married. Arturo had come away
realizing Lydia's vulnerability at the hands of her family:
how her innocence could be manipulated as easily as her
sister's breasts. Seeing how someone so close to her could
be corrupted, he came to hate her sister as if she had personally wronged him.

The boy waited for the fracas of the tanks to pass but
did not lower his volume, nor did he change his opinion.
"Same one. They took turns under the water tower." He
broadcast it with utter candor before the strangers surrounding them, and even quoted the price: "For a ring
with a make-believe ruby."

Arturo tried to remember without success whether she
had ever worn fake jewelry to school. Finally the morbid
urge to unearth the details won out. "So when did this
take place?"

"A month ago. I missed my chance by days."

"It wasn't her, then," said Arturo. "The whole family
goes to California for the summer as soon as school's out."

In his desperation to save her good name, he had ignored the obvious: "Then what's she doing here?" asked
the boy.

Rafa's cousin said, "She must have stayed on to have
the baby." He stared harder and added, "Doesn't she look
a little swollen to you?"

Arturo knew little about such matters but checked her
profile anyway. "It's just baby fat."

The boy laughed. "Of course. The baby's making her
fat." Then, as if it just occurred to him he might be of-
fending someone, he added: "Anyway, it was just a small

gang."

Arturo tried to stare down her accuser when he realized that, in his own way, the boy meant nothing personal
against her or him. So he forced his attention to a gaggle
of senile rednecks on horseback, billed as a retired sheriff's
posse. He even smiled when the boy suggested that their
gaudy outfits and faces mottled by the fierce sun made
them look like transvestites.

The posse left a pile of horse manure in its wake, directly in the path of an approaching band. The boys
held their breaths in anticipation, but somehow the band
marched past and left it intact. Afterwards, with throngs
on each side paying the band indirect homage, almost every adult seemed to stare elsewhere.

Rafa's cousin decided to make the most of the situation and of the firecrackers Arturo had given him. He began tossing them at the horsecake with such gusto that the
rest wanted to join him. Even Arturo seemed interested,
until Rafa's cousin gave him one of his own firecrackers.
Arturo shook his head and was handing it back when the
boy suddenly lit the fuse. He barely had time to throw it
wildly in the street.

The other three burst out laughing. "Hit the target!"
yelled Rafa, then pointed to Arturo's pockets. "If you
don't use them, we will."

"They're for later."

"What later?" asked Rafa. "They're perfect for here."

He was right—they were too small to bother any
bystanders—so Arturo finally joined them.

They continued lobbing firecrackers with the concentration of a carnival crowd pitching coins at souvenir
plates. But Arturo's enthusiasm was extinguished when
he saw Lydia, and behind her the tall man whose crossed
arms made him resemble a somber guardian angel. Even

though she was not looking at him, he suddenly felt child-
ish and ashamed. He stopped and tried to rub off the stink
of gunpowder from his palms.

The rest continued throwing firecrackers at the horse
manure until they ran out of them.

"Anybody got more fireworks?" asked the boy.

Rafa's cousin showed his empty hands then pointed at
Arturo. "I got mine from him."

"Lend me some," said the boy. "I'll repay you when
I'm back on my feet."

Reluctantly, Arturo began tugging out some small firecrackers when a huge one fell out.

"Jesus!" said the boy. "A bomb!" He scooped it up
before Arturo could reach it. "Don't worry," he promised,
then repeated, "I'll pay you as soon as I'm back on my
feet."

"What good is that? By then it'll be over."

"Then I'll pay you back by Christmas." When Arturo
hesitated again, the boy insisted: "I told you, I'm not going back."

"That's not it."

"So what is it?"

"That firecracker's too big. Someone could get hurt."

"Hey, I'm no kid."

He was almost ready to light the fuse when the inspi-
ration hit him: he picked up a discarded miniature flag,
called a cease-fire and ran to the horsecake, where he sank
the little wire pole hilt-deep.

"I don't think that's a good idea," his cousin said when
he returned.

"It's a great idea! It's the country's birthday."

Arturo had his doubts as well, although he could not
tell why. It was not out of a love for his country. That
had always seemed something abstract, the way he was ex-

pected to love his fellow man. Besides, he was old enough to know that America belonged to *los americanos*, and *los americanos* were Anglos.

Still, something about the whole thing bothered him. "If it's such a great idea," he told the boy, "how would you like a shit cake for your birthday?"

For a moment the boy stared at him as if Arturo had insulted him beyond apologies. Then all at once he smiled. "I wouldn't give a shit. And nobody gives a shit about this either." He turned to a pair of young men beside him whose dress and demeanor made it obvious they were undocumented Mexicans. He asked if they objected, then turned back to Arturo. "See?"

He pretended to lob the large firecracker as if he were about to shoot a basketball. Just then his cousin Rafa said:

"A cop!" He pointed to a spot close to Lydia but several people back. A dignified Chicano, head and shoulders above the crowd, was opening a path to the street.

"He's no cop," said the boy. "Check out the cap." He indicated the gold stencil on the man's cap. "He's just a veteran."

"He looks pissed," added Rafa's cousin.

"He can't touch us. We're kids."

Still, he hurried his throw after lighting the firecracker, which nonetheless landed almost in the center of the cake. But the boy's glee immediately turned sour.

"Damn thing's got no bang!" He turned to Arturo, who explained:

"It's got a slow fuse because it's big."

"Bring it over here and let's see."

Arturo washed his hands of the whole thing. "It's not mine anymore."

"Then the deal's off. It's no good, so I don't owe you shit." The boy hoped this would prod Arturo. It did not, so he went over to the horsecake himself. He reached for the firecracker, but the veteran reached him first. The man was still catching his breath to say something when the firecracker suddenly sparkled like a reanimated birthday candle. The boy still had a nonchalant smile on his face when the veteran noticed the live fuse. For an instant the man seemed to relive some horror of combat before he grabbed the boy for cover. Arturo barely had time to glance at Lydia before his instincts followed that of the other boys: he shielded himself behind the bulk of an ample adult just as the cake exploded. A moment later he peeped out from behind his human sandbag and his heart sank. The boy was hugging the patriot now, trembling from the sheer fright of the explosion. They had taken the brunt, but the rest of the stuff had claimed a wide radius. Astonished, Arturo simply said, "Wow!", in a tone that almost claimed credit for the bull's-eye, even though he could not hear himself over the ringing in his head. But he did feel someone tugging at his sleeve, and a moment later he made out Rafa's plea. "Let's get out of here, Turi!"

Rafa was close to laughing and crying at the same time, and Arturo sensed it was the scariest but most exciting moment of his friend's life because he felt the same way. The crowd milled about confused, almost frightened, as if the frail control at its core had disintegrated with the small explosion. People who had stood next to each other now looked at one another with the blankness of absolute strangers. An anxious few made tentative glances at each other as if desperate to come together again. A few more simply examined their arms and clothing for soiled evidence, wondering whether the specks they saw were real or imagined. The uncertainty added to Arturo's anxiety, which shifted back and forth from his stomach to his heart. He looked around for Lydia and found her close to where she had stood earlier, except that her relatives had formed a belated semi-circle in front of her. He gave her a fleeting glance, as ashamed to examine her as if each stood naked before the other. His breathing came in crazy patches now, but the strength in his arms and legs was beginning to ebb, as his muscles seemed nothing more than an imagined excitement.

"Let's go, Turi!" But the pounding of his heart only hammered him deeper to the spot. A part of him told him to stay, to apologize and make amends; but it was a part more anchored in exhaustion and surrender than conviction.

"Damnit, Turi, move! We'll end up in the shade!" All at once his heart and the heat of the day made the decision for him, as the wild pounding catapulted him through the chaos of the crowd.